PLAYS BY

# EDWARD ALBEE

# MALCOLM

# MALCOLM

### ADAPTED BY
## EDWARD ALBEE
### FROM THE NOVEL BY
## JAMES PURDY

NEW YORK 1966

## ATHENEUM

FOR JAMES PURDY

WITH EVER-GROWING ADMIRATION

*January 11, 1966, New York City, Shubert Theatre*

| | |
|---|---|
| MALCOLM | MATTHEW COWLES |
| COX | HENDERSON FORSYTHE |
| LAUREEN | ESTELLE PARSONS |
| KERMIT | JOHN HEFFERNAN |
| A YOUNG MAN | VICTOR ARNOLD |
| MADAME GIRARD | RUTH WHITE |
| GIRARD GIRARD | WYMAN PENDLETON |
| A STREETWALKER | ESTELLE PARSONS |
| ELOISA BRACE | ALICE DRUMMOND |
| JEROME BRACE | DONALD HOTTON |
| GUS | ALAN YORKE |
| JOCKO | ROBERT VIHARO |
| MELBA | JENNIFER WEST |
| MILES | HENDERSON FORSYTHE |
| MADAME ROSITA | ESTELLE PARSONS |
| HELIODORO | VICTOR ARNOLD |
| A MAN | WILLIAM CALLAN |
| A WASHROOM ATTENDANT | HENDERSON FORSYTHE |
| A DOCTOR | HENDERSON FORSYTHE |
| VARIOUS PEOPLE | VICKI BLANKENSHIP |
| | JOSEPH CALI |
| | WILLIAM CALLAN |
| | ROBERT VIHARO |

*Directed by* ALAN SCHNEIDER

*Designed by* WILLIAM RITMAN
*Costumes by* WILLA KIM
*Lighting by* THARON MUSSER
*Music by* WILLIAM FLANAGAN

# ILLUSTRATIONS

# MALCOLM AND HIS FRIENDS

## AN ALBUM

PHOTOGRAPHS BY ALIX JEFFRY

THE BEGINNING—Malcolm with Professor Cox

Malcolm with Kermit—the oldest man in the world?

LEFT TO RIGHT—Eloisa Brace; two Malcolms; Jerome the burglar

LEFT TO RIGHT—Malcolm; Madame Rosita, his teacher; Gus, former husband of Malcolm's wife-to-be; Miles, a man who resembles Professor Cox

Malcolm with his wife, Melba, a well-known singer

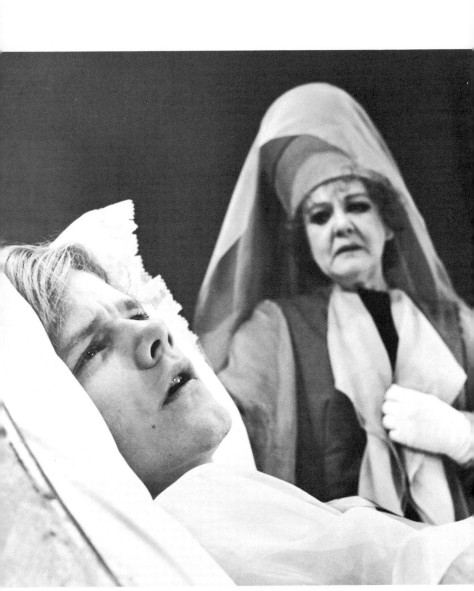

THE END—Malcolm dies, observed by Madame Girard

# ACT ONE

# SCENE ONE

(*A golden bench;* MALCOLM *seated on it; no expression save patient waiting.* COX *enters, behind* MALCOLM, *grimaces, stands for a moment, hands on hips, tapping his foot, finally advances*)

COX

(*Rather petulantly*) You seem to be *wedded* to this bench. (MALCOLM *smiles, does not look at* COX, *but, rather, down at the bench*) You!

MALCOLM

(*Looks up; a sweet smile*) Oh, I'm here all the time. (*Tiny pause*) My name is Malcolm.

COX

(*A trifle edgy*) Good morning; my name is Cox. (MALCOLM *smiles, nothing more;* COX *pauses a moment, then*) I suppose, of course, you *are* waiting for somebody; your sister, perhaps.

MALCOLM

(*His attention slipping away*) No. (*Then back*) I'm waiting for nobody at all.

COX

(*Impatient; suspicious*) You have such a waiting *look*; you've been here for*ever*. For months and months.

MALCOLM

(*Surprise*) You've seen me?

COX

Of course I've seen you; this is my . . . I, I walk by here
every day.

MALCOLM

Oh. Well, in that case, I suppose I *am* waiting for somebody.

COX

(*Helpful; after* MALCOLM *says no more*) Yes?

MALCOLM

(*Statement of fact*) My father has disappeared.

COX

Well, don't tell me you've been waiting for *him* all this time.

MALCOLM

(*Thinks for a moment; then*) Yes; perhaps I may be waiting
for *him*. (*Then he laughs, openly, agreeably*)

COX

(*Snorts*) Waiting for your father!

MALCOLM

I'm afraid I have nothing better to do.

COX

Ridiculous! I've taken special notice of you, because nobody
has ever sat on this bench before. I don't think anybody
*should* sit on it, for that matter.

MALCOLM

(*Firmly; clearly enunciated*) Poppycock.

COX

(*Dogmatic*) I am speaking of the regulations. This bench was
set out here in front of the hotel as decoration, to . . . to

set things off, and I don't . . .

MALCOLM

(*No apology*) Well, I am a guest in the hotel and I sit where I please.

COX

(*Miffed*) I see! (*Tiny pause*) It's clear you've not heard of me. (*Clears his throat*) I am an astrologer.

MALCOLM

(*Innocent delight*) People still study the . . . stars . . . for, for . . . ?

COX

(*Snort of disgust*) People!

MALCOLM

(*Gentle apology*) I'm sorry.

COX

(*Regarding* MALCOLM *carefully, appraisingly*) Do you have no one, then?

MALCOLM

(*As if the question were odd, unfamiliar*) No one?

COX

No one.

MALCOLM

(*Clearly dropping the above*) I'd invite you to sit down, sir, but you quite clearly don't think it should be done, and I wouldn't want to ask you if you didn't want to do it.

COX

(*Intentional bored tone*) Your way of refusing to give information?

MALCOLM

Things are, well, a bit too much for me, you see: I'm quite young, I guess. So I sit here all the time . . . I suppose.

COX

Guess!? Suppose!? You *know!*

MALCOLM

(*A sweet smile*) Well, sir; yes; I know.

COX

(*Broods*) Hmmmmmmmmm.

MALCOLM

(*A fact*) I suppose, though . . . that if someone would tell me what to do, I would do it.

COX

(*Regards him; chooses his words carefully*) Would that be wise, though? For someone so young?

MALCOLM

(*Finally touching the bench with his hand, to emphasize a point*) If I could leave the bench . . . if I saw some purpose . . . I would risk it.

COX

(*Relieved, energized; takes a notebook and pencil from his pocket*) Good. When were you born, Malcolm? The date of your birth. (MALCOLM *is silent*) Don't tell me you don't know!

MALCOLM

(*Quite simple about it*) I'm afraid you're right: I don't.

COX

Then I don't see how you expect me to help you.

MALCOLM

(*Quietly confused*) Help . . . sir?

COX

(*To himself*) I don't think I've ever met anybody who didn't know when he was born.

MALCOLM

But since he—my father—disappeared, I've had nobody to remind me of dates.

COX

How *old* are you? Do you know *that?* V*aguely?*

MALCOLM

(*Sweet smile*) I'm . . . I'm afraid not, sir.

COX

(*Regarding* MALCOLM *closely*) You look really quite young. Well, are you . . . have you . . . do you, uh, have . . . hair?

MALCOLM

Sir?

COX

(*Embarrassed*) Hair. Do you have hair, uh, under your arms, and, uh. . . .

MALCOLM

(*A winning smile; laughs*) Oh. Yes. Recently.

COX

Ah, well, then, you are probably . . . Did your father never talk to you about plans? Plans for when you were grown up?

MALCOLM

(*Hesitant*) Grown . . . up?

COX

*(Gloomily)* Grown up.

MALCOLM

*(A little sadly)* No. *(Rather tentative, then growing in pleasure)* My father . . . my father seemed to feel I was always going to stay just the way I was, and that he and I would always be doing just about what we were doing *then*. We were both satisfied. You have no idea, Mr. Cox, sir. *(A faint frown)* We were very happy together, my father and I.

COX

Well, for God's sake, Malcolm, you're not happy now!

MALCOLM

*(Quite level)* No, sir; I'm not.

COX

Well, you've got to do something about it!

MALCOLM

Do?

COX

Yes; *do*.

MALCOLM

*(A quiet appeal)* But, what is there to do?

COX

You must . . . give yourself up to things.

MALCOLM

*(Rises, a little apprehensive)* Give myself up to . . . things?

COX

Of course, my dear boy. You must begin your education.

MALCOLM

But, my father taught me . . .

COX

Your education to *life*, Malcolm!

MALCOLM

Sir?

COX

Since you are going out into the world—leaving your bench, so to speak—you must prepare yourself. You have the look of innocence, Malcolm . . . and that will never do!

MALCOLM

No, sir?

COX

Innocence has the appearance of stupidity, my boy.

MALCOLM

It does, sir?

COX

Yes, the two are easily confused, and people will take the easy road, Malcolm, and find you stupid. Innocence must go! (*Softer*) And I can help you; I can give you people, if you think it's people you're looking for . . . addresses.

MALCOLM

(*Confused*) Addresses, sir?

COX

Addresses. That is, if you want to give yourself to things—to life, as an older era said.

MALCOLM

Well, I have no choice, have I. But . . . addresses?

COX

(Hands MALCOLM *a calling card; uses his lecturer's voice*)
Here is the first. I want you to take this card, and you are to
call on the people whose names are written on it, *today*, at
five o'clock.

MALCOLM

(*After folding his arms, and a long pause*) I will *not!* I will do
no such thing. (*Then, suddenly he takes the card and studies
it, then reacts with consternation. Intense displeasure*) Kermit
and Laureen Raphaelson indeed! (*Throws the card on the
ground*) I'll have nothing to do with such an absurd introduc-
tion. You must be . . . out of your mind.

COX

Pick up that card at once! What would your father think of
you!

MALCOLM

Kermit and Laureen Raphaelson indeed!

COX

If you do not obey me . . . I will never speak to you again!
(*Scoffs*) Sitting there, day after day, moping over your father,
who probably died a long time ago . . .

MALCOLM

Disap*peared*, sir.

COX

(*Pushing on*) Yes, and when help for you arrives in the shape
of an address, what do you want to do! Nothing! You prefer to
stay on that bench. You prefer that to . . . *beginning*. . . .

MALCOLM

(*Reconsiders*) Well, I will do as you say in this one case.

COX

You will do as you're told, since you don't know what to do at all.

MALCOLM

(*A gentle smile*) Very well, sir.

COX

And remember the exact hour: five.

MALCOLM

Yes, sir.

COX

(*As he leaves*) Remember, Malcolm . . . you must *begin.*

MALCOLM

(*Looking at the card*) Yes, sir . . . begin.

COX

You'll rather enjoy Kermit and Laureen, I think . . . they're children—like yourself.

MALCOLM

(*Disappointed*) Oh? Yes?

COX

Grown-up children. (*As he exits*) Remember, Malcolm. . . . You must *begin.*

# ENTRE-SCENE

*(*MALCOLM *leaves the bench scene, which changes in darkness. He comes forward, broods some, then speaks to his father, rather as if they were standing together)*

MALCOLM

Dear father . . . I am to begin. Begin what? I don't know, but . . . something. My education, I believe. Oh, father; I miss you so very much, and I don't understand . . . at all: why you've left me, where you have gone, if you *are*, as they say, dead or if you will ever return. I miss you so. But I am to begin now, it would appear, and I will try to be all you have taught me . . . polite; honest; and . . . what is the rest of it, father? That you have taught me? *(Looks at card)* Do you know . . . do you know Kermit and Laureen Raphaelson, father? By chance, do you know them? Grown-up children, father?

# SCENE TWO


*(The lights come up on the set of the Raphaelsons' house.* LAUREEN *is in it. She calls to* MALCOLM*)*


### LAUREEN
Malcolm? Hurry up, now. Over here.


### MALCOLM
*(Moving tentatively into the set)* Uh . . . yes. You're . . . uh, Laureen Raphaelson?


### LAUREEN
Oh, *am* I. And you! You *are* Malcolm; you *are* from Professor Cox.


### MALCOLM
Uh . . . yes, I suppose.


### LAUREEN
Kermit is not with us at the moment, as you can see.


### MALCOLM
Well, no . . . , I . . .


### LAUREEN
As a matter of fact, he's in the pantry finishing his supper. He eats in there alone now quite often, just to spite me, I think. I'm afraid Professor Cox may be right . . . that we're headed for the divorce courts. What do you think of that?


### MALCOLM
Divorce courts are entirely out of my range of experience. But

I'm sorry you're headed for them.

LAUREEN
(*Thinking it over*) I haven't said divorce is actually imminent, mind you.

MALCOLM
No?

LAUREEN
Though it probably is. My God, you're young, aren't you? (KERMIT *enters;* LAUREEN *sees him*) There he is, Malcolm. It's Kermit! There's Kermit. (*To* KERMIT, *very eager to please*) You have a caller, Dolly.

MALCOLM
(*Observing* KERMIT, *open-mouthed, as he advances*) Why, who are *you?*

KERMIT
(*Rather amused, but slightly imperious*) Who am I? You heard her. I am Kermit. *Her* husband. Oh, I can't tell you how glad I am to see somebody nice for a change, and stop looking so surprised, Malcolm, you are Malcolm, right?

MALCOLM
Why . . . uh, yes. . . .

KERMIT
Why don't you just ignore Laureen there, and pay proper attention to *me?* After all, I'm the lonely one.

LAUREEN
Good God alive, it's beginning already. I beg you, Kermit: don't bring on a scene in front of this child.

KERMIT
(*Settling into a chair*) So . . . you are the boy who is infatuated with his father.

MALCOLM

I? Infatuated?


LAUREEN

Professor Cox has already told us all about you.


MALCOLM

But there's nothing to tell . . . yet.


KERMIT

(*Gravely*) There is always a great deal to tell, Malcolm, as I have learned.


MALCOLM

(*To break a stared-at feeling*) And you really *are* married.


KERMIT

*She* proposed.


LAUREEN

I warn you, I will not tolerate your telling secrets about our marriage to a third party again. Ever!


KERMIT

(*To* MALCOLM; *proudly*) I am the oldest man in the world.


LAUREEN

(*Familiar argument*) You are not!


KERMIT

I most certainly am!


LAUREEN

You most certainly are not!


KERMIT

(*To* MALCOLM) I am one hundred and ninety-two years old.

LAUREEN

You are no such thing!


KERMIT

(*To* LAUREEN) I am one hundred and ninety-two years old.


LAUREEN

You're ninety-seven years old . . . (*Mutters*) for God's sake.
(*Louder*) You're not even one hundred.


KERMIT

I'm much too old to argue with you. (*Back to* MALCOLM)
Why did you decide to come to see us, Malcolm?


LAUREEN

(*To herself*) One hundred and ninety-two years old indeed!
(*To* MALCOLM; *something of a challenge*) Yes, why did you
come?


MALCOLM

Why did I come to see you? Why, Mr. Cox ordered me to.


LAUREEN

Professor Cox has ruined Kermit here with his ideas. Kermit
and I were *so* happy before we met that awful man.


KERMIT

(*Laughs derisively*) Laureen, sweetheart, if you're going to
start a sermon, I'll have to ask you to leave the front room
and go out and sit in the back parlor with the cats.


LAUREEN

(*Rather steely for all-suffering*) You should tell Malcolm how
many cats you have out there so he can have a picture of
where you're ordering me to go. (KERMIT *makes a little face;*
MALCOLM *stifles giggles*) We have fifteen cats! Malcolm, am
I getting across to you?

#### KERMIT

*(In confidence, to* MALCOLM*)* Professor Cox has a rather low opinion of Laureen at the moment.

#### LAUREEN

He has a low opinion of everybody, I would suspect. *(Turns to* MALCOLM*)* Malcolm, sweetie, do you know what Professor Cox suggested to me, only last week? *(*MALCOLM *shakes his head)* But you're too young to hear it! Oh, God! So terribly young, and unaware.

#### KERMIT

Nonsense! No one's too young to hear anything about people! And where's my hot tea, by the way? I asked you for my tea nearly an hour ago.

#### LAUREEN

*(Hastening to the tea table)* Dolly, didn't I bring you your tea? I won't have it said I've neglected my duties by you, no matter what may happen later on. Malcolm, honey, will you join Kermit in a cup of tea?

#### MALCOLM

*(Very little boy)* Yes, please.

#### KERMIT

*(As* LAUREEN *brings the tea)* Just what *did* Professor Cox command you, Laureen? Why don't you regale us with it?

#### LAUREEN

*(Giving* MALCOLM *his tea, kissing him on the cheek, ignoring* KERMIT's *last remark)* Here, precious.

#### MALCOLM

Thank you, Laureen. Yes, what did Mr. Cox command you?

#### KERMIT

*I'll* tell you what Mr. Cox commanded her.

###### LAUREEN

(*Put upon*) Let me tell it, Kermit; I want the boy to hear it without your embellishments.

###### KERMIT

Will you allow me to entertain *my* guest in *my* fashion? I am one hundred and ninety-two years old.

###### LAUREEN

You are not.

###### KERMIT

(*To* MALCOLM) We are poor people. (*To* LAUREEN) Quiet! (*Back to* MALCOLM) And knowing my wife's *propensities,* a long history we need not go into here, Professor Cox merely and sensibly proposed that Laureen go out with certain gentlemen who would pay her for her compliance with their wishes, since she was not entirely unknown for her favors before her sudden proposal of marriage to me. (*To* LAUREEN) Silence! (*Back to* MALCOLM) Laureen had promised when she proposed marriage to me and I had agreed to be her husband that my days of struggle and difficulty would be over. (*To* LAUREEN, *as if she were threatening to speak*) YES? (*Back to* MALCOLM) The exact opposite, alas, has been true. Since the prolonged weekend of our honeymoon in Pittsburgh, there has not been a day . . .

###### LAUREEN

(*Quite the tragedienne*) When one's husband no longer respects one, when he can tell the most intimate secrets of a marriage in front of a third party, there is, indeed, nothing left for one but the streets. Malcolm, baby, do I look like a streetwalker? (*Goes right up to him, towers over him*) Answer me, dear boy, for you're not yet corrupt. (MALCOLM *does not answer*) Do I . . . or don't I?

###### MALCOLM

(*Quite confused*) But aren't you . . . already one, dear Laureen? I . . . I thought your husband said you . . .

KERMIT

*(Laughs uproariously)* Go back there and talk to the cats; I want to be with Malcolm. Go on! I certainly deserve to see somebody else in the evening besides your own horrible blonde self.

LAUREEN

*(Disdainfully, at* KERMIT*)* A true pupil of Professor Cox. *(Kisses* MALCOLM *benevolently, retires without looking at Kermit again.)*

KERMIT

*(Shouting after her)* Back with the other alley cats! *(Laughs pleasantly)*

MALCOLM

Are there really cats back there?

KERMIT

As Laureen said: there are fifteen.

MALCOLM

What an extraordinary number of cats.

KERMIT

Well, I've been collecting them for a while. After all, I'm one hundred and ninety-two years old.

MALCOLM

How . . . how odd that Laureen should be a . . . a . . .

KERMIT

*(Quite conversationally)* Odd she's a whore? Well, it's the only thing she ever wanted to be, and why she thought marriage would straighten her out, especially marriage with *me*, God only knows.

MALCOLM

I don't seem to recognize women like that when I meet them.

KERMIT

You *do* have beautiful clothes.

MALCOLM

Do I? (*Looks down at himself*) They're all suits my father picked out years in advance of my being this size. He's picked out suits for me all the way up to the age of eighteen. I think he had a presentiment he'd be called away, and he left me plenty of clothes.

KERMIT

(*More polite than anything*) Your father was quite extraordinary.

MALCOLM

(*A little whine in the voice*) That's what I tried to tell Mr. Cox, but he wouldn't believe me. I'm . . . I'm glad you think my father was extraordinary. (*Surprisingly near tears*) You see, he's all I've got . . . and now I don't have him. (*A few brief, genuine sobs*)

KERMIT

(*After a decent interval*) You have *me*, Malcolm; I'll be your friend.

MALCOLM

(*Recovering; a sweet smile*) Thank . . . thank you, Kermit.

KERMIT

I'll be your friend.

MALCOLM

You . . . you have beautiful clothes, too.

KERMIT

*(Modest)* Oh, well, they're . . . they set me off.

MALCOLM

I've . . . I've never met anybody as old as you are, before.

KERMIT

Well, you haven't met many people, have you, Malcolm?

MALCOLM

No. There's one thing, though, I must get straight. Are . . . are you really as old as you say you are?

KERMIT

*(Tossing it off with a little laugh)* Well, of course.

MALCOLM

But you can't be!

KERMIT

*(Quite petulant)* Why not?

MALCOLM

Well . . . nobody *could* be!

KERMIT

*(Straight curiosity)* Do you want me to tell you about the Boston Tea Party?

MALCOLM

Uh . . . no. (KERMIT *sticks his tongue out at* MALCOLM) Golly, you look awful when you do that.

KERMIT

*(Offhand)* I *am* awful sometimes.

MALCOLM

I think I like you, though; you're not usual.

KERMIT

Well, I could say the same thing of you, Malcolm, but I won't. Not that I don't like you; I do—but that you're unusual. You're not bright, I gather, but you have your own charm, an air of . . . innocuous fellowship.

MALCOLM

(*Solemnity and awe*) Aren't you . . . afraid? I mean . . . well . . . being so old and all . . . aren't you afraid of . . . dying?

KERMIT

(*After a mouth-open pause, quite casually calls*) Uh, Laureen? Laureen?

MALCOLM

I'm, Im sorry if I . . .

KERMIT

Laureen?

LAUREEN

(*Enters, examining her hand*) One of your damn cats bit me. I think it was Peter. Honestly, Kermit, I wish you'd do something about . . .

KERMIT

Laureen, Malcolm just said the oddest thing.

MALCOLM

I'm sorry, Kermit, really I am.

LAUREEN

(*Still with her hand, barely interested*) Yeah? What did you say, Malcolm?

KERMIT

(*As if it were funny*) Malcolm asked me if I wasn't afraid of dying.

LAUREEN

*(Only the mildest, matter-of-fact criticism, offhand)* Oh, you shouldn't say anything like that, Malcolm.


KERMIT

*(Just a hint of self-reassurance)* When I was your age, Malcolm, the idea of death occurred to me, and I was very frightened.


LAUREEN

I mean, that isn't a nice thing to say at all.


KERMIT

And I lived with it all through my forties and fifties and everything, and by the time I was a hundred or so . . .


LAUREEN

You're ninety-seven. I don't see why we can't get rid of those damn cats.


KERMIT

. . . by the time I was a hundred or so . . . I'd resigned myself to it.


LAUREEN

It just isn't a nice thing to say to anybody, Malcolm.


KERMIT

But on my one hundred and forty-fifth birthday the idea suddenly hit me that there wasn't any death. So when I was a hundred and eighty-five I married Laureen here . . .


LAUREEN

I mean, when you're dealing with a person who's over ninety and all, I . . . I just don't see why you want to scare me like that.

KERMIT

. . . and we have each other, and the cats, and everything. . . .


LAUREEN

I don't think you know how to behave around grownups,
boy.


KERMIT

Malcolm doesn't know what life is, Laureen; he just doesn't
know, that's all.


MALCOLM

Well, no, I . . . I suppose I don't.


LAUREEN

You come back and see us, Malcolm, some other time. (*Beginning to stroke* KERMIT) We wanna be alone for a little
now. You'll understand when you're married. We got our
own problems, Kermit, being ninety-seven and all. . . .


KERMIT

One hundred and ninety-two.


LAUREEN

But you call us. Call us now, you hear?


MALCOLM

Yes, well . . . thank you both for the evening. Thank you
for . . .


KERMIT

(*Enjoying being fondled etc.*) Come back and see us, Malcolm. Come back and see *me*. I'm the lonely one.


MALCOLM

Yes, I . . . good, goodnight to both of you.

LAUREEN

Goodnight, baby.

KERMIT

I'm your friend, Malcolm, no matter what you think of me. Who knows, I may be your only friend in the world. You can cry here any time.

LAUREEN

Oh, Dolly, you're wonderful, you really are. So wonderful.

*(As this set fades, as* MALCOLM *moves away)*

KERMIT

*(Cheerfully)* I'm one hundred and ninety-two years old.

LAUREEN

*(Teasing him)* You are not.

KERMIT

*(A tone creeping in)* I am one hundred and ninety-two years old!!

LAUREEN

Dolly, you are *not* a hundred and ninety-two years old.

# ENTRE-SCENE

(MALCOLM *backs away from the Raphaelsons' as it fades to blackness.* MALCOLM *is alone*)

MALCOLM

Love . . . Love is . . . *Marriage* is . . . Married love is the strangest thing of all. (*More or less to his father*) Of everything I have seen, married love is the strangest thing of all. (COX *enters, unseen by* MALCOLM)

COX

What are you doing, Malcolm?

MALCOLM

(A *smile, self-assurance*) Thinking aloud.

COX

Thinking what?

MALCOLM

(A *recitation*) That married love is the strangest thing of all.

COX

(*Stern*) Not true!

MALCOLM

(*Quiet smile*) Ah, well.

COX

I was talking with my wife only last night.

MALCOLM

(*Astonishment*) You mean there is a *Mrs.* Cox?


COX

(*Rather sniffy*) Of course! Everybody is married, Malcolm . . . everybody that counts.


MALCOLM

(*Dubiously*) I don't understand why Laureen won't admit that Kermit is one hundred and ninety-two years old.


COX

(*Hedging*) Well, she has a certain personal right to deny it, if she wishes to. Besides, maybe he isn't.


MALCOLM

Well, Kermit was very firm about it.


COX

That is so like Kermit!! The day will come . . . the day will come when Laureen will have to admit that Kermit is one hundred and ninety-two years old, or Kermit will have to admit that he isn't.


MALCOLM

You mean they can't both go on believing what they want?


COX

(*A flicker of kindness*) Well, not if they're the only ones who believe it.


MALCOLM

(*Sad glimmer of knowledge*) Aaaahhh.


COX

(*All business again; takes card from his wallet*) Well, here

is your second address, Malcolm. Society, great wealth, position, sadness.

MALCOLM

*(Rather sadly)* So soon.

COX

*(Brandishing, presenting a card as if on a platter)* The Girards. Madame Girard, and her husband. You must hurry,
though. The Girards are very wealthy people, and while the
very wealthy have no sense of time, their interests do . . .
shift, the portals close, the beautifully groomed backs . . .
turn . . . no loss . . . but yours.

MALCOLM

*(Looking at the card)* Mr. and Mrs. Girard . . . "The Mansion."

COX

*(Moving off)* Hurry to them; hurry now.

MALCOLM

*(To the retreating* COX*)* Maybe . . . maybe they've met . . .
maybe they'll know where my father is!

COX

*(Exiting)* Ah, well . . . if your father exists, or has ever
existed . . . perhaps they will. *(Exits)*

# SCENE THREE

MALCOLM

*(Alone for a moment; the Girard set will light directly. Great bewildered wonder; to himself)* If he exists . . . or has existed! If he exists! *(To his father, now)* Do you know them, father? . . . Mr. and Mrs. Girard, who live in the mansion? Are very wealthy, have great position, and have . . . beautifully groomed backs—and fronts, I would venture? *(Laughs, joyously)* Is that where you are, father? Will you be waiting for me there?

*(A* YOUNG MAN *appears)*

YOUNG MAN

Are you Malcolm?

MALCOLM

Oh! Uh, yes, sir, I am.

YOUNG MAN

I thought you were; you look like you should be. Come along now. Madame Girard is demanding a settlement from her husband; you're just in time for the evening performance.

MALCOLM

A settlement? Of what sort?

YOUNG MAN

Money, of course! Divorce. What are settlements for? *(Shrugs)* Peace at the end of wars, settlements, money, what else? Come now.

*(They enter the Girard set.* MADAME GIRARD *is*

*seated on a throne of sorts.* GIRARD GIRARD *stands
near her, another* YOUNG MAN *to the other side of
her.* MADAME GIRARD's *make-up is smeared all over
her face; she is drinking; is drunk)*


MADAME GIRARD

*(As the* YOUNG MAN *ushers* MALCOLM *into her presence)*
Who admitted this child? *(Takes a drink)*


GIRARD GIRARD

Why, Professor Cox called up, my dear, and asked if this
young man could not be received. *(Goes to* MALCOLM, *hand
out)* Good evening, Malcolm.


MALCOLM

*(After difficulty getting his hands out of his pockets, shakes
hands with* GIRARD GIRARD) Good, good evening, sir.


MADAME GIRARD

*(To her husband)* And who gave you leave, sir, to accept
invitations by proxy for me? I have a great mind to take
proceedings against you, to in*crease* the settlement, proceedings with reference to the matter we discussed earlier in the
evening.


GIRARD GIRARD

*(Sotto voce)* Please try to be more hospitable, Doddy.


MADAME GIRARD

Don't use pet names for me in front of strangers! *(Points to*
MALCOLM) You! Come here. (MALCOLM *advances,* MADAME
GIRARD *looks him over carefully)*


MALCOLM

Is my . . . my tie straight?


MADAME GIRARD

*(Wonder and sadness)* Heavens! You can't be more than six

years old. (*To* GIRARD GIRARD, *peremptorily*) Get him a drink. (GIRARD GIRARD *moves to do so*)

MALCOLM

(*To* MADAME GIRARD) Are . . . are all of you friends of Mr. Cox? (*The four* YOUNG MEN *laugh and exchange knowing glances*)

MADAME GIRARD

(*Glowering at her husband*) Why is it you're not entering into the spirit of the party? Do you want me to begin proceedings against you at once? (*The* YOUNG MEN *giggle*) Well!?

GIRARD GIRARD

(*Giving* MALCOLM *his drink*) Now, Doddy.

MALCOLM

(*To* GIRARD GIRARD) I had no idea it was going to be like this.

MADAME GIRARD

What is *it*?

MALCOLM

(*With some distaste*) Your party, or . . . gathering, or whatever you call it.

MADAME GIRARD

(*Drinking again*) We are here . . . for the sole purpose of taking proceedings against my husband—boor and lecher— seducer of chambermaids and car hops. . . .

GIRARD GIRARD

(*So patiently*) Now, Doddy . . .

MADAME GIRARD

(*To* MALCOLM, *still*) And I think I can arrange this settle-

ment quite properly without comments from the newly arrived and half-invited.


###### MALCOLM

*(Rather loud and self-assertive)* Perhaps *Mr.* Girard may
want a divorce first!
*(The* YOUNG MEN *laugh,* GIRARD GIRARD *smiles quietly)*


###### MADAME GIRARD

Newly arrived and *un*-invited!


###### MALCOLM

*(Is he a little drunk himself? Still rather loud. Genuine con-
cern)* You must drink a *great* deal, Madame Girard.
*(Again, guffaws from the* YOUNG MEN*)*


###### MADAME GIRARD

*(Crafty, eyes narrowing)* What was it you said, young man?


###### MALCOLM

I think you are intoxicated, Madame.
*(Great laughter)*


###### MADAME GIRARD

*(Drunk dignity)* Do you realize in whose mansion you are?


###### MALCOLM

Why, Mr. Girard's mansion.


###### MADAME GIRARD

Clearly you do not.


###### MALCOLM

*(To the others)* This is only the second place I've visited at
Mr. Cox's request, but I can't say it's the more pleasant or
comfortable of the two.

MADAME GIRARD

Hear him!? He's not a guest—he's a critic! Not only a critic, but a spy! Throw him out! THROW him OUT!!

GIRARD GIRARD

Doddy; *dear.*

MADAME GIRARD

A filthy spy for that vicious old pederast!

GIRARD GIRARD

Doddy, not in front of a child.

MALCOLM

*(Fascinated)* Old what? Ped . . . what? What did she call him?

GIRARD GIRARD

Doddy, please. *(To* MALCOLM*)* I believe I've heard mention of your father.

MALCOLM

*(To* GIRARD GIRARD, *with wonder and hope)* You really knew my father!

GIRARD GIRARD

Ah, no; I said, I believe I've heard mention of him.

MADAME GIRARD

*(An announcement) I* . . . do not think your father exists. *(Takes a great gulp)* I have *never* thought he did. *(*MALCOLM *swallows, stares at her open-mouthed)* And what is more . . . *(Takes another drink)* . . . *nobody* thinks he exists . . . or ever *did* exist.

MALCOLM

That's . . . that's . . . blasphemy . . . or, a thing above

it! (MADAME GIRARD *laughs, echoed by the* YOUNG MEN) And
. . . *(Quite angry now)* . . . this is the first time where I
have ever attended a . . . a . . . *meeting* . . . a meeting
where the person in charge was *drunk!* (A *strained tiny silence*)

### MADAME GIRARD

Oh, my young beauties, see how I'm suffering. *(Stretches out
her hands to the* YOUNG MEN, *who take them)* Come and
comfort me, beauties.

### MALCOLM

*(An aside to* GIRARD GIRARD) What a pretty face she must
have under all that melted make-up.

### MADAME GIRARD

Oh, dear God, I've been through so much; nobody knows
what I've suffered. *(Whimpering)* And now with this spy
here from Mr. Cox; he'll go directly back to that old pederast and tell him *everything* about this evening. . . .

### MALCOLM

Old *what?* Pederast?

### MADAME GIRARD

How I was *not* at the top of my form, and Cox will call his
clients and tell *them* I was not at the top of my form, and
they in turn will call . . .

### GIRARD GIRARD

*(Solicitously)* Would champagne help?

### MADAME GIRARD

*(Weeping a little)* Yes; it would help a little; a lot might
help a little. (GIRARD GIRARD *motions to one of the* YOUNG
MEN, *who fetches champagne)* It's so hard to bear one's burdens sometimes, and we don't *need* MALCOLM, do we? *(Re-*

*fers to the* YOUNG MEN) And haven't I my young beauties around me already. Aren't they enough? Do we need a paid informer? A paid informer in the shape of this brainless, mindless . . . (*Suddenly as if seeing* MALCOLM *for the first time*) . . . this *very* beautiful young boy?

MALCOLM
(*Sort of drunk; flattered, childishly "with it"*) Perhaps we should all drink to Madame Girard.

MADAME GIRARD
My dear, dear young friend. Oh, thank you. Leave Mr. Cox, dearest Malcolm; be mine; be my own Malcolm, not his.

MALCOLM
Let's all drink to Madame Girard!

MADAME GIRARD
(*Approaching him, putting her hands on him, kissing his cheek, etc.*) Do you know, my young, my very young dear friend, the company you've been keeping? Do you know what Mr. Cox *is?*

MALCOLM
(*Raising his glass, in a gleeful toast*) A pederast!

ALL THE OTHERS IN UNISON
WHAT!?

MADAME GIRARD
(*A bemused smile*) What word did I hear? What word, Malcolm? Did you say something?

MALCOLM
(*Draining his glass*) I don't intend to repeat myself. My father never did. Hurrah!

MADAME GIRARD

Champagne! Champagne for everyone; a prince has come among us! Royalty!


GIRARD GIRARD

Champagne! Champagne!
> *(The scene will start fading now . . . swinging off, whatever. Everybody is talking at once. But above it all we hear . . .)*


MADAME GIRARD

Royalty! Real royalty! A prince has come among us! A true prince!

# SCENE FOUR

(*Kermit's.* KERMIT *alone in his set.*)

MALCOLM
(*Enters*) Kermit—Kermit, I've been to the Girards'.

KERMIT
Poor Kermit; poor little man; poor poor little man.

MALCOLM
(*Nodding, embarrassedly*) And . . . and they've accepted
me and . . .

KERMIT
I knew you wouldn't fail me . . . as much as one can know
anything. Laureen has left me . . . the bitch has up and
taken off.

MALCOLM
(*Sympathizing*) Left *you.*

KERMIT
(*Bitterly*) Oh, what's so surprising about that? (*Grabbing*
MALCOLM's *hand, weeping freely*) She left me all alone,
Malcolm.

MALCOLM
I . . . I . . . (*Shrugs sadly*)

KERMIT
Oh, I'll grant I hadn't really *loved* Laureen in . . . months;
she'd lost her sparkle, and there were times when she almost

disgusted me, but I'd got so *used* to her, her waiting on me, her . . . her being *around*. I'm . . . all alone now.


MALCOLM

Did she . . . did she run off with somebody?


KERMIT

(*Anger coming back*) How else would she go!? Like a decent human being? Alone? Of course not! She ran off with a Japanese wrestler!


MALCOLM

(*Terribly puzzled*) But . . . how did she find one?


KERMIT

I don't know!


MALCOLM

(*Softly, to solace*) Was he—the Japanese wrestler—also very old?


KERMIT

He was the . . . usual age for a man.


MALCOLM

It's pretty scary, isn't it, being alone?


KERMIT

We're both alone, you and I. Aren't we lucky Professor Cox brought us together? We're both in an impossible situation.


MALCOLM

Certainly *I* am.


KERMIT

(*Quite put out; after a tiny pause*) Why you more than I?

MALCOLM

Well, you *have* something; your marriage, which means you know *women*. I have . . . nothing; there's nothing I can *do*. All I have is the memory of my father. My father . . .

KERMIT

(*Quivering with rage*) SHIT ON YOUR FATHER!! (*Total silence.* MALCOLM *slowly rises.* KERMIT *slowly comes over to him, tugs at his sleeve*) Malcolm! Forget I ever said that. (MAL-COLM *moves away a few feet*) You just listen to me, and for-give me. You must let me apologize, dear, dear Malcolm.

MALCOLM

(*Removed, sort of lost*) How can I ever listen to you *again*? And how can I forgive you? To have said *that* about my father! This is the very last straw of what can happen to me. I'm going to pack up and leave the city today!

KERMIT

You have no right to desert me or, for that matter, desert your father. He . . . he may come back for you. Malcolm, my entire world has gotten out of bed and walked away from me. I'm depending on you so! I have no one else to depend on.

MALCOLM

A likely story coming from a man who insults the dead . . . the *disappeared*.

KERMIT

Forgive me, Malcolm, I only meant irritation. There you were, talking on and on about your father, and I wanted to talk about *my*self, and about the whore of a wife . . . (*Begins sniffing*) . . . who I miss so much. . . .

MALCOLM

(*Rather kingly*) Very well, then, Kermit, you're forgiven for this once.

KERMIT

Laureen, Laureen, Laureen . . .


MALCOLM

(*Shyly*) Kermit? Why did Laureen really leave you?


KERMIT

(*Sighs*) It was so strange. At exactly the same minute I decided to tell her I was only ninety-seven, to make it easier
for her, she walked into the room, looking sort of funny, saying she'd decided to live with the fact that I was a hundred
and ninety-two. And so we argued about it for a while, me
insisting I was only ninety-seven, and she telling me that I
was older than hell itself, and then she said she couldn't
take it any more, and . . .


MALCOLM

How . . . how old are you? Really?


KERMIT

Hm? Oh . . . well, I don't remember any more. I'm up
there, though . . . two . . . two hundred and something.


MALCOLM

I . . . I like you, Kermit. I like you very much.


KERMIT

Yes? Well, come and see me soon, Malcolm. I'm really very
lonely now.

# ENTRE-SCENE

(MALCOLM, *between sets, alone, stands, shakes his head a little, sadly, suddenly sees, leaning against the proscenium, a* STREETWALKER *who looks like Laureen, is played by the actress who plays Laureen, false wig, too much make-up, ridiculous dress.* MALCOLM *walks toward her, slowly, mouth open*)

### MALCOLM

Why . . . why, *Laureen.* (*The* STREETWALKER *pretends not to notice him; he speaks now somewhat as if he were punishing a naughty child*) *Laureen!* You go home at once! Shame on you, leaving Kermit like that.

### STREETWALKER

(*Bored, tough, not a parody, though*) What do *you* want, kid?

### MALCOLM

Laureen, it's Malcolm.

### STREETWALKER

Laureen!? My name's Ethel.

### MALCOLM

Why, it is not! Your name is Laureen Raphaelson, and you're married to Kermit Raphaelson, who is a terribly old man, at least one hundred and ninety-two years old and maybe two hundred and something . . .

### STREETWALKER

(*Nodding her head as if* MALCOLM *were insane*) My name is

Laureen Raphaelson, and I am married to a terribly old man
at least one hundred and ninety-two years old and maybe
even two hundred and something.


MALCOLM

Yes, and you've left him and you've run off with a Japanese
wrestler, and I think you ought to go home right this minute.


STREETWALKER

(*Nodding her head even more*) My name is Laureen Raphaelson, and I am married to a terribly old man who is at least
one hundred and ninety-two years old or maybe even two
hundred or something except that I've left him and run off
with a Japanese wrestler.


MALCOLM

(*Quite stern, oblivious of her incredulity*) Yes, and I think
you ought to go home right this minute.


STREETWALKER

(*Ponders this a little*) And where is this Japanese wrestler
right now?


MALCOLM

(*Flustered for a moment*) Why . . . why, wrestling, I'd
imagine.


STREETWALKER

Uh huh. I think you better go home yourself, kid.


MALCOLM

No! I think you had. (*Whines*) Laureen . . . please.


STREETWALKER

(*Shakes her head*) Amazing. I thought my name was Ethel,
and I thought I was not married, save once, a long time ago,
for a couple of weeks to a nice kid turned out was a fag and

is now shacking up with a cop picked him up one night in
a bus depot, very happy I believe, stays home, cleans the gun,
cooks . . .

MALCOLM

(*Whining*) Laureeeeeeeeeeeeen!

STREETWALKER

You got a family, kid?

MALCOLM

(*Struck by her question*) A what? A family?

STREETWALKER

Mommy? Daddy?

MALCOLM

I . . . I *had* a father, but he . . .

STREETWALKER

(*Soberly, not unkindly*) Died?

MALCOLM

(*Nods, solemnly*) Uh . . . yes, it would seem.

STREETWALKER

Gee, I thought your name was maybe something like Donald
or Malcolm, and you lived in a big hotel, except your money
was going, and your father wasn't dead, but had only . . .
disappeared. Not dead . . . gone away.

MALCOLM

Yes! That's *right*. Disap*peared*.

STREETWALKER

(*Walking slowly toward off*) You better get home, kid;

Mommy and Daddy spank they find you out late, talking to
. . . grownups.

MALCOLM

My father isn't dead! He only disap*peared!*

STREETWALKER

Good for you, baby, better go home to Daddy . . . *(Exits)*

MALCOLM

Laur . . . ! *(Pause; softly; alone)* Not dead . . . only gone
away. I didn't mean to say that you were dead, father, but
you've been . . . disappeared so long, and everybody says
. . . I'm sorry, father, but please come back . . . so it won't
be true.

*(Begins to move toward the set of his bedroom in
the hotel, which begins to light)*

# SCENE FIVE

(*Malcolm's hotel bedroom; old, stately furniture.* GIRARD GIRARD *is there, his back to the audience.* MALCOLM *enters, not from a door, but right onto the set*)

MALCOLM

(*Deep in thought, takes off coat, does not see* GIRARD GIRARD *at first, then*) Why . . . (GIRARD GIRARD *turns around*) . . . why, Girard Girard! What are *you* doing here?

GIRARD GIRARD

My dear Malcolm, my dear boy, I hope you'll forgive me waiting for you in your own bedroom, but I had to see you, and . . .

MALCOLM

(*Rather put off*) But how did you get in here?

GIRARD GIRARD

(*Kindly*) Getting here was no problem, Malcolm; I own the hotel, and as for *why* I am here . . .

MALCOLM

(*Sniffing*) Well, if you own the hotel, I should think you'd do something about the water pipes: there's rust and it takes ages for the hot water to come.

GIRARD GIRARD

It's an old place, Malcolm, a great one, but old. Besides, when I told you I owned the hotel I didn't mean to suggest that I managed it as well. It is a . . . property, a . . . something that's passing through my portfolio.

MALCOLM

(*Quite formal*) So much for the how, sir; but what of the why? *Why* . . . are you here?

GIRARD GIRARD

If I've disturbed you, I'm deeply sorry, but my coming is dictated by an emergency.

MALCOLM

(*Concerned*) Nothing serious? Madame Girard hasn't taken ill, or died?

GIRARD GIRARD

Madame Girard is at home, sleeping in her private wing of the mansion.

MALCOLM

(*Quiet wonder*) Private wings. Indeed, that *is* an extension of separate rooms, is it not?

GIRARD GIRARD

It is indeed. I've come here to make a very unusual suggestion to you, and I hope you'll hear me out. And I want to make it very clear to you that I've come here on my own volition, despite the fact that Madame Girard herself ordered me to come. Madame Girard has taken such an immediate and violent fancy to you that we wondered—and please don't think us too outrageous—we wondered if you'd care to come with us to our chateau for the summer.

MALCOLM

(*Pacing for a moment*) Why, I'm speechless with surprise at your generosity. It's . . . overwhelming.

GIRARD GIRARD

You have no idea how . . . pleased Madame Girard would be, Malcolm.

MALCOLM

No, sir; of course I haven't.


GIRARD GIRARD

And since you will make both me and my wife very happy
if you will come with us to our chateau for the summer, we
may expect you?


MALCOLM

. . . No, sir.


GIRARD GIRARD

But, Malcolm!!


MALCOLM

(*Ponders it, then*) You see, I'm terribly afraid of leaving here
where I'm always alone, and waiting, and going to where
people may demand me at all hours . . .


GIRARD GIRARD

(A *little less patiently than before*) No one will demand anything of you that you don't want to give.


MALCOLM

. . . and then there is the bench.


GIRARD GIRARD

The bench, Malcolm?


MALCOLM

It is where I receive my addresses, sir! Where I have made
contact . . . with *people*, sir. And there is Kermit, sir . . .


GIRARD GIRARD

Kermit? Kermit?


MALCOLM

(*Slow and very serious*) My very best friend in the world, I think; one person whom I could never leave.


GIRARD GIRARD

(Sigh of relief) Well, then bring him with you—bring your
Kermit with you.


MALCOLM

(Almost thinking aloud) Perhaps . . . if Kermit were to
come . . . perhaps, then, I could accept.


GIRARD GIRARD

(Last lollipop) You could have one of the gatehouses, if you
liked . . . anything!


MALCOLM

(Very sincere) I will try very hard, sir.


GIRARD GIRARD

(So gentle) That is all we ask. Come spend the summer with
us; be our son.


MALCOLM

Be like your son, sir.


GIRARD GIRARD

(As he prepares to leave the set; wistfully) Between simile
and metaphor lies all the sadness in the world, Malcolm.


MALCOLM

(As GIRARD GIRARD turns, starts to leave) It does, sir?


GIRARD GIRARD

Do let us know; come with us; be ours.


MALCOLM

(Nods; not an acquiescence, but a pondering) Yours.

#### GIRARD GIRARD
(*Leaving*) Goodnight, Malcolm.

#### MALCOLM
(GIRARD GIRARD *has left*) Good—goodnight, Mr. Girard . . . sir. (COX *enters from left*—KERMIT *enters from right on his chair on treadmill*) Kermit, we are going to the chateau for the summer. We are going with the Girards.

#### KERMIT
The Girards . . . the chateau . . .

#### COX
(*To himself*) Oh, I wouldn't count on that, buddy, if I were you. I wouldn't be so sure about that at all.

#### MALCOLM
We're on our way, Kermit.

#### COX
I wouldn't count on anything in this whole damn world.

#### MALCOLM
We're on our way, Kermit. We're on our way. (*Exits*)

# SCENE SIX

(*Kermit's sitting room, but rearranged, this time, so that when Kermit is facing his front door, his back will be to the audience.* COX *standing,* KERMIT *sitting, his knees together, his hands clasped on them*)

COX

I suppose you think you're going to go. (*No answer from* KERMIT) I said: I suppose you think you're going to go. (KERMIT *looks up, but does not speak; his eyes are near tears*) Is there to be a long parade? . . . of all of you? . . . all my students, all whom I've raised from nothing, you, Malcolm, God knows who else? . . . streaming after that pied piper of a Girard woman . . . like rats?

KERMIT

(*A weak whisper*) Mice?

COX

(*Intimidating, loud*) HM? WHAT?

KERMIT

(*Clears his throat; a tiny voice*) Mice. Pied piper: mice. (*A little malice now*) Rats leave a sinking ship.

COX

(*Choosing to ignore it*) All of you, whom I've educated beyond your state, risen up so that you can look at life, if not in the eye, at least at the belt buckle? All of you, running off? No thank you, sir! (KERMIT *says nothing*) Hm? HM?!

KERMIT

(*Still cowed*) I have been asked . . .

C O X

SPEAK UP!!

K E R M I T

I have been asked.

C O X

*(Fuming, to himself)* It is the fate of sages and saints, I suppose, to serve, teach . . . *give,* if you will, of their substance . . . and be abandoned in the end, left desolate on the crag, like our beloved Francis, while the mice, the *rats,* scurry off . . . playing in the great gardens, nibbling at the pâté, the mousse . . . garnering.

K E R M I T

*(So timid, apologetic)* I have . . . been asked.

C O X

*(Looks at* KERMIT *carefully, changes his tack a little)* Well, yes, of course you have, my fine fellow . . . asked.

K E R M I T

Yes!

C O X

*(Comforting a child)* Of course! And you want to go.

K E R M I T

*(The wonder is too much for him)* The . . . Girards . . .

C O X

The Girards? Yes?

K E R M I T

*(Blurting it out)* The Girards have invited me to the chateau and it would be wonderful. I'd see nice people . . . and everything might be all right there.

COX

*(A vicious confidence)* Now look here, I don't mind playing games, but the time comes we gotta get serious, right?

KERMIT

Right.

COX

You're very special, a very special person; you're fragile, Kermit, and your eyes aren't strong; you couldn't stand the . . . grandeur. . . . You'd be blinded by the splendor, Kermit.

KERMIT

*(Breathes the word with loss and awe)* The . . . splendor.

COX

It'd knock your eyes out, kid; you couldn't take it.

KERMIT

Then I . . . I can't go?

COX

Unh-unh.

KERMIT

I can't go with Malcolm to . . . to the chateau, with Madame Girard and . . .

COX

Unh-unh.

KERMIT

*(Knowing it's all up)* But I'd be so happy there.

COX

You couldn't take the splendor, kid; I'm sorry.

KERMIT

*(As* cox *starts to leave, but not by the front door; off to one side)* I would have been so happy there, with Malcolm, and . . .

[MALCOLM, GIRARD GIRARD *and* MADAME GIRARD *will come on-stage and move to Kermit's front door*]

COX

*(Exiting)* Whatever happens, Kermit, don't let them in. Remember, the splendor. *(Exits)*

MALCOLM

*(To the* GIRARDS, *as* KERMIT *huddles within)* . . . and he told me on the phone he washed the walls with ammonia and scented it all with patchouli oil and rosewater, which are your favorites for a dwelling, are they not, Madame Girard?

MADAME GIRARD

They are essential for a habitation. *(Squints)* What a charming little building; you must buy it for me, Girard.

GIRARD GIRARD

All right, Doddy.

MADAME GIRARD

I smell cats!

GIRARD GIRARD

*(Some wonder)* Do you, Doddy?

MALCOLM

*(Eager glee)* There are fifteen!

KERMIT

*(Huddled in a corner; whispers to himself)* Go away, oh, do go away.

MALCOLM

(At the front door) Kermit? Hello?

KERMIT

(Not heard by the others) Go away . . . please.

MALCOLM

(Knocks) Ker-mit. (No answer; tries the doorknob) He . . .
he doesn't answer.

MADAME GIRARD

Nonsense! (She tries it, too) Why doesn't he answer? Is he
expecting us?

MALCOLM

Of course! Kermit? Don't play games with me.

GIRARD GIRARD

Perhaps your friend is indisposed.

MADAME GIRARD

When we are visiting? Don't be absurd. (MADAME GIRARD
enters imperiously, followed by MALCOLM and GIRARD GIRARD)
Do you hear me, my good man? It is I, Madame Girard! I am
issuing a command! You are coming with us to the country.

KERMIT

(Shaking his head, sobbing) I can't; I . . . cannot.

GIRARD GIRARD

Here, let me try.

MADAME GIRARD

(Motioning him away) You can't do anything; I have the
splendor here.

MALCOLM

Kermit! Please! We're going to the chateau! Don't be a

coward; come with me; I can't go without you!

KERMIT

(*A trapped animal, very loud*) Go away! I . . . can't bear the splendor!

MALCOLM

(*Whining a little*) Kermit!

MADAME GIRARD

What is it you can't bear?

KERMIT

(*Shouting*) I can't stand the splendor of your presence!

MADAME GIRARD

(*Awe and joy*) The *splendor* of our presence!

MALCOLM

(*As above*) Kermit, please!

KERMIT

(*Moans*)

MADAME GIRARD

Why, the creature is moaning! (*At which* KERMIT *moans louder*) He is moaning . . . over *us!*

MALCOLM

(*Loss*) Kermit? . . . Please?

KERMIT

(*Weeping to himself*) I . . . I can't. I cannot.

MALCOLM

(*Intensity*) Kermit! (*The three wait for a little, in silence, the only sound being* KERMIT'S *sobbing as he and his chair slide off*)

MADAME GIRARD

*(Finally, softly)* Well, then, we shall have to go without him.
Girard?

GIRARD GIRARD

It would seem so, Doddy. I'm sorry, Malcolm, you shall have
to come with us without your friend.

MALCOLM

*(Soft, loss)* Kermit!

MADAME GIRARD

*(As they all begin to move away from Kermit's door)* Kermit
has rejected me.

MALCOLM

It's *me* he has rejected.

MADAME GIRARD

*(Patiently)* He has rejected *all* of us. I must have a drink.

MALCOLM

*(Rather severe)* What of?

MADAME GIRARD

*(Sweetly, patiently explaining)* Dark rum.

GIRARD GIRARD

Completely out of the question.

MADAME GIRARD

Explain the meaning of that last remark.

GIRARD GIRARD

Your drinking days are over. At any rate, with me around.

MADAME GIRARD

You pronounce my doom with the sang-froid of an ape! You
are an ape!

GIRARD GIRARD

I warn you, Madame Girard, I'm at the end of my tether.
We must leave for the country at once; my lungs demand
the air. Malcolm? You shall have to come with us . . .
alone.

MALCOLM

I can't, Mr. Girard, sir; I can't abandon Kermit now.

GIRARD GIRARD

(*Sad shrug*) Alas.

MALCOLM

(*Rueful agreement*) Yes; alas.

MADAME GIRARD

(*Bravura cheerfulness*) We have tried and failed. (*Puts her
hand out*) Lead me, Girard.

GIRARD GIRARD

Goodbye, Malcolm?

MALCOLM

Goodbye, Mr. Girard, sir; goodbye, Madame Girard.

MADAME GIRARD

(*Being led off by* GIRARD GIRARD) Goodbye, dear child, dear
ungrateful child. (*They both exit*)

MALCOLM

(*Rather petulant*) Well, you've made rather a hash of things,
I must say, Kermit. A whole summer, two people who loved
me, or so they said, a man like Mr. Girard who said he would

be like my father—all of it, everything, for *both* of us, and you won't do it! *(Tapping his foot, rather impatient)* Well? What's to become of me now? I hope you've got plans for me. I've given up everything for you! *(But* MALCOLM *is alone. Frightened little boy)* What's to become of me?

# ENTRE-SCENE

(cox *comes on, sees* malcolm *alone*)

cox

(*Feigning surprise*) What? You still here? Lucky boy, aren't you off with the tycoon and his lady, and where is your friend Kermit?

malcolm

(*Surly*) You study astrology and things, don't you?

cox

(*Shakes his head*) Tch-tch-tch-tch-tch; up the ladder too quick, down they plunge to the bottom rung, as the saying goes. Arrogant, weren't you, crowing over your triumph and all?

malcolm

(*A front*) It's . . . it's just a matter of a day or two, until I get things settled here, and then I'm off.

cox

Good thing, too, I must say, since your room is gone, your bags out in front of the hotel. Checked out, have you?

malcolm

Of course! I . . . (*Bursts into tears*) What am I to do? It was all arranged, and then Kermit lost his courage and said he wouldn't go, and . . .

cox

Tears? What would your father, or whoever it is, or was, say? Hm?

MALCOLM

*(Trying to stop crying)* And where has Kermit gone, and what's *wrong* with him?


COX

*(Quite casual)* Kermit, I'm sorry to say, is probably going to have a nearly complete collapse.


MALCOLM

*(Wonder with the stopping tears)* A nearly complete collapse?


COX

Yes, poor little man; the presence of the unattainable often brings one on.


MALCOLM

*(Great wonder)* Poor Kermit.


COX

Yes, but poor Malcolm, too, poor of pocket as well as other resources.


MALCOLM

My bags . . . you say . . . were . . .


COX

*(Jolly)* Out on the curb. Empty, though.


MALCOLM

But my clothes! My shells! My . . .


COX

*(Jollier)* Sold, whisked off, taken in payment, gone.


MALCOLM

*(Great awe)* And what am I to do!?

COX

(*Bringing out another card*) Start lower, I think; ascend again. Oh, you should count yourself lucky I bother with you at all.

MALCOLM

(*Some spunk left*) Should I! Well, let me tell you, everyone in and out of the Girards' speaks slightingly of you.

COX

(*Coolly*) Those in possession of the truth are hardly ever thought well of.

MALCOLM

(*Some awe*) You are in . . . possession of the . . . truth?

COX

(*Calm, with a small smile*) I thought you knew I had it.

MALCOLM

Then, you *are*, as people say, a magician as *well* as an astrologer.

COX

(*Tossing it off*) I merely try to help—sometimes I fail, as in your case, child. You are very difficult to educate. (*Handing* MALCOLM *a card*) Here. Take it.

MALCOLM

(*Some enthusiasm*) *Another* address, sir?

COX

Not so much enthusiasm, Malcolm. What did your father— such as he was or was not—teach you?

MALCOLM

(*Ingenuous*) To be polite, sir, and honest.

COX

(A *little sour*) Your father spoke in contradictions, then.


MALCOLM

Sir?


COX

These people . . . be cautious.


MALCOLM

(*Genuine alarm*) But why are you sending me to them, Mr. Cox, sir!?


COX

(A *great shrug*) What is left for you, Malcolm? Maybe you're on the way down, for good; maybe not. 'S'up to you. Besides, it's the only card I happen to have with me. (*Starts to go*) Goodnight, kiddie.


MALCOLM

(*Looks above, sees it has gone dark*) Why . . . it *is* night.


COX

Yes, gets dark pretty quick around here, don't it?


MALCOLM

(*Still amazed*) Yes; very. (*Sees that* COX *is leaving*) Mr. Cox!


COX

Hm?


MALCOLM

(*Real anger*) I don't understand your world, Mr. Cox, sir! Not one bit!


COX

You will, sonny, you will. (*Walks offstage, leaving* MALCOLM *alone*)

# SCENE SEVEN

*(Eloisa Brace's studio begins to light.* ELOISA *is in it, in the growing light. There is distant jazz music going on)*

MALCOLM

*(Half calling after* cox, *half talking to himself)* Not a bit of your . . . world, Mr. Cox, sir, not one little bit. Caution? How do I do that?

ELOISA

*(Having listened to* MALCOLM*)* O.K., kid; all right, O.K. All right?

MALCOLM

*(Startled to see her)* Oh! My goodness.

ELOISA

You the new kid, hunh? Malcolm? Is it you? *(*MALCOLM *nods)* Practicing caution?

MALCOLM

Is that what I'm doing? Are you . . . ?

ELOISA

O.K., then, either come in or go out. You can't just stand there, O.K., you know? I'm giving a concert.

MALCOLM

*(Enthusiasm)* Are you!

ELOISA

I'm Eloisa Brace, O.K.?

MALCOLM

How do you do? Mr. Cox . . .


ELOISA

(*Irritable*) Yeah, yeah, O.K.


MALCOLM

(*Entering the set*) You're awfully cross tonight, aren't you?


ELOISA

Look, buddy, if you had a bunch of musicians lying around the house . . .


MALCOLM

I'm sorry!


ELOISA

Yeah? O.K. Hey! I'm gonna paint your portrait. (MALCOLM *only smiles a little*) I said: I'm gonna do a picture of you. Paint. O.K.?


MALCOLM

Are . . . are you a painter?


ELOISA

(A *little suspicious*) I don't know where we're gonna put you while you're living here, every bed in the damn place is full of musicians and all, but you look pretty small, we'll find part of a bed for you. O.K.? My God, I hate kids how old are you!


MALCOLM

Well, I think I must be fifteen by . . .


ELOISA

O.K.! There's that face of yours, I'm gonna paint. (*Rather mysterious*) It's like a commission: I mean, I think I can sell it right away I got it done. O.K.?

MALCOLM

O-O.K.


JEROME

*(Entering)* Is that the new boy? *(Sees* MALCOLM*)* Ooh, yes, it does look to be.


ELOISA

Will you please take over from here, O.K.? You know I can't stand kids, and I got all these musicians waiting.


JEROME

*(Rather sweet, urging her out)* O.K., baby.


ELOISA

*(To* MALCOLM, *as she exits)* I gonna paint the hell out of you, kid. O.K.?


MALCOLM

*(As she goes)* Y-yes . . . certainly.


JEROME

*(Taking* MALCOLM *by the arm, walking him further into the set)* My wife is a bit nervous when we have these concerts.


MALCOLM

*(Astonished)* Eloisa Brace is *your* wife?


JEROME

*(Nods)* Oh, yes. *(Leads* MALCOLM *further)* But do come clear into the room, why don't you—where I can see you.


MALCOLM

*(Uncertainly)* Sure.


JEROME

*(Looking at* MALCOLM *carefully)* Yup, you're just as Mr. Cox

described you. Yup. *(Nods several times)* Would you like some wine, Malcolm?

MALCOLM

*(As a glass is being poured for him)* I usually don't drink.

JEROME

*(Hands* MALCOLM *a glass, takes one himself)* Do have some.

MALCOLM

You're so . . . very polite.

JEROME

*(Returning the compliment)* You're much nicer than I even thought you would be for a boy of your class. My name, by the way, is Jerome. *(They shake hands. Hope and enthusiasm in his voice now)* I don't suppose you've heard of me. I'm an ex-con, a burglar. You're not drinking up. *(Pours* MALCOLM *more wine)*

MALCOLM

*(Rather drunk, vague)* But you see . . . I don't drink. Jerome, what *is* an ex-con?

JEROME

A man who's been in prison. An ex-convict.

MALCOLM

Ah; I see!

JEROME

I wrote a book about it.

MALCOLM

How *difficult* that must have been!

JEROME

*(Going to get a copy)* Would you like to read my book?

MALCOLM

Well, I . . . I don't know; I've . . . I've never read a complete book—all the way through.

JEROME

(*Leering some*) You'll read this one. (*Hands it to* MALCOLM) It's called *They Could Have Me Back.*

MALCOLM

(*Looking the book over*) What a nice title. Is that you naked on the cover? (JEROME *smiles, touches* MALCOLM *lightly on the ear*) I . . . I don't read very much.

JEROME

(*Touches* MALCOLM *gently on the ear again*) Do you dig that music, kid?

MALCOLM

(*Touching his ear where* JEROME *had touched it*) What did you do that for?

JEROME

(*Pouring* MALCOLM *more wine*) Look, Malcolm, I know you make a point of being dumb, but you're not *that* dumb. (JEROME *sits at* MALCOLM's *feet, his arm around his leg, his head against his knee*) I *do* want you to read my book; I want you to, well, because, because I guess you don't seem to have any pre-judgments about anything. Your eyes are completely open. (MALCOLM *jumps a little as* JEROME *starts stroking his thigh*) Look, Malcolm, I'm not a queer or anything, so don't jump like that.

MALCOLM

(*Drunk, vague*) I see.

JEROME

Will you be a good friend, then?

MALCOLM

*(From far away)* Of course, Jerome.


JEROME

Thank you, Malcolm. It's going to be a wonderful friendship. *(Strokes some more)* But I think you better give up Girard Girard and Mr. Cox and all those people, because they don't believe in what you and I believe in. . . .


MALCOLM

*(Very dizzy)* But what do we believe in, Jerome?


JEROME

What do we believe in, Malc? What a lovely question, and you said we; I'll appreciate that for one hell of a long time. One hell of a long time from now I'll think of that question of yours, Malc: What do *we* believe in? You carry me right back to something. . . .


MALCOLM

*(The jazz music is louder,* MALCOLM's *head spins)* But you see, I don't know what I believe in, or any . . .


JEROME

Don't spoil it, Malc! Don't say another word!


MALCOLM

*(A tiny voice; he is about to pass out)* Jerome . . .


JEROME

Don't say a word, now. Shhhh . . . *(At this moment the glass falls out of* MALCOLM's *hand, and he topples from the chair, head first, across* JEROME's *lap)* Jesus Christ! Malc? *(Shakes* MALCOLM, *but he has passed out)* MALC?

*(Lights fade on the tableau)*

# SCENE EIGHT

*(Eloisa Brace's studio again.* ELOISA *and* COX *swing on, with portrait, etc.)*

ELOISA

Well, whatta ya think of the portrait, hunh?

COX

It's . . . it's . . . very interesting.

ELOISA

*(Put out)* Oh? Really?

COX

I mean . . . it's beautiful.

ELOISA

I thought that's what you meant.

COX

It's lovely, my dear.

ELOISA

It has a certain . . . *him* about it, don't you think?

COX

Well, that depends on what you mean, Eloisa. It doesn't look exactly like *him*—or he doesn't look exactly like *it*. . . . Maybe it's a picture of what he used to be . . . or what he's becoming.

ELOISA

*(Her leg is being pulled)* Ooohhh . . . you astrologers, you're something.

COX

*(Down to business)* I happened—just in passing, you understand—to mention the portrait of Malcolm to Madame
Girard.

ELOISA

*(Going along with it)* Just in passing.

COX

Yes, and she seemed—well, how shall I put it?—she seemed
beside herself.

ELOISA

*(Feigned lack of interest)* Oh? Yes?

COX

Ah. How we dissemble.

ELOISA

I can't imagine what you're talking about.

COX

Madame Girard finds herself in the curious dilemma of, on
the one hand, feeling that Malcolm is the most ungrateful
child who ever lived, and, on the other hand, retaining for
the boy—or, to put it most accurately, for the fact of him—a
possessiveness that borders on mania.

ELOISA

*(More openly interested)* Oh, really?

COX

Yes; and when I mentioned to her that you were painting his
portrait, her eyes flashed with the singular fire that's the ex-
clusive property of the obsessed.

ELOISA

*(Tiny pause)* Meaning?

COX

Meaning simply that Madame Girard will stop at nothing to have Malcolm's portrait. That I think you've got a big sale coming.

ELOISA

(*Knowingly*) Yeah? And?

COX

And that I hope you'll not forget my commission.

ELOISA

(*Airily*) Oh, Professor Cox, you'll have your ten percent.

COX

(*Clears his throat*) Uh, twenty.

ELOISA

(*Steely*) Fifteen.

COX

Agreed.

MADAME GIRARD'S VOICE (*offstage*)

Eloisa Brace? Eloisa Brace?

COX

Aha! You see? I think I'll go out this way, if you don't mind.

MADAME GIRARD'S VOICE

Eloisa Brace?

COX

And leave you two ladies to your business.

ELOISA

(*Fact, but no judgment*) You're a terrible man, Professor Cox.

COX

(*Exiting*) Yes? Well, do keep in the back of your mind that
the role of a post-Christian martyr is not an easy one.


ELOISA

(*As* cox *exits*) A post-Christian martyr!


MADAME GIRARD

(*Entering*) Eloisa Brace? It is I!


ELOISA

(*Feigned surprise*) Why, Madame Girard!


MADAME GIRARD

I'm lonely, my dear.


ELOISA

Well, sure you're lonely, but . . .


MADAME GIRARD

You have a young man named Malcolm here, and don't pre-
tend you've not.


ELOISA

Why, yes! I'm painting his portrait.


MADAME GIRARD

Oh? Then I must buy it at once! I've not been so taken with
a person in years.


ELOISA

(*Drinking, or pouring brandy*) But, lady, I haven't finished it
yet, and . . .


MADAME GIRARD

What are you doing?

ELOISA

I'm sipping brandy.

MADAME GIRARD

At nine-thirty in the morning?

ELOISA

You upset me so, Madame Girard, as you well know, and sometimes a finger of brandy helps me get through.

MADAME GIRARD

I know nothing of your anxieties. All I know is Malcolm is here and you are painting his portrait. *I* discovered *him,* and *I* claim *it.*

ELOISA

Madame Girard! Listen to reason!

MADAME GIRARD

I am claiming my own is all. If that is decent brandy, I might just have a taste.

ELOISA

Oh, please! You know we buy only a cheap domestic.

MADAME GIRARD

*(Sniffs with displeasure)* Well, naturally, what can one expect?

ELOISA

Why don't you just toot along, Madame Girard? Your wealth and position don't entitle you to come into a private house and . . .

MADAME GIRARD

*(Snorts)* A public house, from what I've heard! The things you've done to that sweet, though ungrateful child.

ELOISA

Like what!

MADAME GIRARD

(*Momentarily stopped*) Well, you have *done* something to
him, haven't you?

ELOISA

Well, it's a little crowded around here—what with musicians
coming and going at all hours—and there aren't enough
*beds*, so Malcolm gets shifted around sometimes, in the
middle of the night—you know, from bed to bed and all,
and sometimes we gotta put *three* people in one bed. . . .

MADAME GIRARD

Three! People!

ELOISA

(*Puzzling it through*) Yeah; Malcolm said it was like travel-
ing in Czechoslovakia during a war. Though how Malcolm
could know that, I can't imagine.

MADAME GIRARD

I'm glad for his own sake that Malcolm's father, or whatever he was, died or whatever he did.

ELOISA

There you go: your middle-class prejudices coming out. Everybody's gotta begin sometime. (*Exits*)

MADAME GIRARD

Eloisa! Eloisa Brace!
(MALCOLM *enters, sees* MADAME GIRARD)

MALCOLM

Madame Girard!

MADAME GIRARD

Are you all right, dear child? Loss? What have they done
to you?


MALCOLM

Not . . . not much.


MADAME GIRARD

Have you kept your innocence! Oh, Malcolm, have they
*used* you?


MALCOLM

Well, it *is* a little crowded when it comes to bedtime, and
I suppose I've . . .


MADAME GIRARD

*(Envelops him)* Oh, my dear child!


GIRARD GIRARD

*(Entering) Monstre!* Take your hands off Malcolm at once!


MALCOLM

Mr. Girard!


MADAME GIRARD

Is that you, Girard Girard?


GIRARD GIRARD

It is I, Madame Girard.


MALCOLM

How . . . how wonderful.


MADAME GIRARD

*(Still sweet)* Why aren't you in the midst of one of your
adulteries, Girard Girard?

GIRARD GIRARD

I have been in Idaho, Madame Girard, making six million dollars.

MADAME GIRARD

You said you would be in Iowa, making four.

GIRARD GIRARD

You misheard me, then, when I told you where I was going and to what end.

MADAME GIRARD

All I can believe is what the detectives say is so.

GIRARD GIRARD

And all I can believe, Madame Girard, is what my wits tell me is so.

MADAME GIRARD

(So sweet) Then I have the better of it, Girard Girard.

GIRARD GIRARD

This once, my dear, I think it is I.

MADAME GIRARD

(After a tiny pause) Oooooooohhhh?

MALCOLM

(To GIRARD GIRARD) I'm so glad to see you!

GIRARD GIRARD

(Not too unpleasantly) Be quiet, Malcolm.

MADAME GIRARD

Why are you here, Girard Girard?

GIRARD GIRARD

I have come for something of great value.

MADAME GIRARD

Yes? As have I! And you shall not have it, sir!

GIRARD GIRARD

I am in the habit of finding my desires satisfied, Madame Girard.

MADAME GIRARD

Oooohhhh, are you ever!

GIRARD GIRARD

But since I find you here, let me speak of a related matter. Do you remember, Madame Girard, that night, so long ago, when we sat in the dark woods, near the lagoon, by the Javanese temples . . . ?

MADAME GIRARD

When I gave you your victory, Girard Girard? The night I surrendered myself to your blandishments and agreed to become your wife?

GIRARD GIRARD

That very night.

MADAME GIRARD

I recall it. I gave up . . . everything, my life, in return for but one thing, which now I cherish: my name—Madame Girard.

GIRARD GIRARD

It is that which I propose to take from you now.

MADAME GIRARD

(*After a pause*) I do not think . . . I hear you well.

GIRARD GIRARD

I have decided, my dear, upon reflection, to give you the

separation which you have demanded without cease since the melancholy day of our marriage.

MADAME GIRARD

Certainly, sir, you will let me determine the relationship between what I wish and what I say I wish.

GIRARD GIRARD

(*Doom-ridden*) No longer! I am divorcing you, Madame Girard.

MADAME GIRARD

(*Haughty*) You will do no such thing, sir.

MALCOLM

Please.

GIRARD GIRARD

Listen carefully to what I say: I am divorcing you, Madame Girard; I am marrying Laureen Raphaelson.

MALCOLM

Laureen Raphaelson!

MADAME GIRARD

That slattern.

GIRARD GIRARD

I am taking your name from you, the name I gave you many years ago.

MADAME GIRARD

You have taken many things from me, Girard Girard: my youth, my job, my self-respect, but there is one thing you may never take from me—my name.

GIRARD GIRARD

You may have the mansion and the chateau, and wealth

enough to satisfy your every whim. I will take but two
things: myself and your name.

MADAME GIRARD

Never, sir!

GIRARD GIRARD

You are history, Madame Girard; you no longer exist.

MADAME GIRARD

(*After reflection*) I will die, Girard Girard; I shall take my
life.

GIRARD GIRARD

I think not, madame.

MADAME GIRARD

(*Very genteel*) But what will become of me? (*Loud*) YOU PIG!

GIRARD GIRARD

(*A little weary, a little sad*) You will move from the mansion
to the chateau, and from the chateau back. You will sur-
round yourself with your young beauties, and hide your
liquor where you will. You will . . . go on, my dear.

MADAME GIRARD

Girard Girard!! The name!! The name is mine!!

GIRARD GIRARD

No longer, my dear. You are history. And now I think I
shall obtain what I came here for.

MADAME GIRARD

Never, sir!! You may not have everything!!

GIRARD GIRARD

Is that a rule, madame? (*Calls, begins moving off*) Eloisa

and Jerome Brace? Are you there? It is I, Girard Girard.

MADAME GIRARD

*(Moving off in the opposite direction, taking Malcolm's portrait with her)* Eloisa! Eloisa!

GIRARD GIRARD

It is I, Girard Girard. *(Exits)*

MADAME GIRARD

Eloisa? Eloisa Brace? *(Exits, leaving* MALCOLM *alone onstage)*

MALCOLM

Girard Girard, sir! Madame Gi . . . everything . . . everything I touch is . . . each place I go, the . . . the, THE WHOLE WORLD IS FLYING APART!! The . . . the whole world is . . . Have . . . have I done this? Is . . . is this because of me? I've . . . I've been polite, and honest, and . . . I've *tried.* I don't understand the world. No, I don't understand it at all. I feel that thing, father . . . Loss. Loss . . . father?

# SCENE NINE

*(Still Eloisa Brace's studio, immediately following.* ELOISA *precedes* JEROME *onstage)*

ELOISA

*(Shrugs)* O.K. *(Calls)* Uh, Malcolm, baby!

JEROME

How's the old Malc!?

MALCOLM

*(Patient, but confused)* I'm *fine*, Jerome.

JEROME

*(False heartiness)* Well, good, kid!

ELOISA

*(Hating to start)* Uh . . . Malcolm . . .

JEROME

*(Coming to her aid)* Malc, we think it's time you were moving on, boy.

MALCOLM

Moving? On?

JEROME

*(False heartiness)* Sure, you don't wanna spend your life in a place like this, buncha jazz musicians, concerts going on, lotta drinking and all, you wanna . . . you wanna go be with your own type, Malc.

MALCOLM

But . . . don't you like me here? (*Looks from one to the other*) I mean, where would I go?

JEROME

Oh, that's all set, kid. . . .

ELOISA

Malcolm, Jerome and I have come into quite a bit of money . . . and we're gonna close up shop for a couple 'a months, an' . . . take a little trip. You know? O.K.?

JEROME

(*As* MALCOLM *is silent*) Fact is, Malc, Madame Girard got what she came for . . .

ELOISA

. . . your portrait, sweetheart . . .

MALCOLM

(*Confused*) She . . . she really wanted the picture?

JEROME

Well, she must of, kid; I mean, that lady right next to you there is happy possessor of the check for the sale of one portrait of someone looks very much like you.

ELOISA

(*Patting her bodice*) Ten thousand dollars, Malcolm. I am, next to Madame Girard, probably the happiest woman on God's green earth.

MALCOLM

(*Amazed*) Ten . . . thousand . . . dollars?

ELOISA

(*Blushing*) Yup!

MALCOLM

*(Doubt on his face, and confusion)* For . . . that *painting?*

ELOISA

*(Ire rising)* Well, some people think my brushwork is worth a great deal more than others, it would appear.

MALCOLM

*(Lying nicely)* I didn't mean *that,* Eloisa; it's a . . . it was a lovely painting.

JEROME

Ten thousand bucks lovely, Malc.

MALCOLM

*(Thinks a moment, then)* Wow.

ELOISA

And Jerome's come into a little money, too, himself.

JEROME

*(Blushing)* Aw, you don't have to mention that, baby. . . .

MALCOLM

Do . . . do you paint, too, Jerome?

JEROME

*(Explaining away something a little shady)* Well, no kid, not that, I . . . well, you see, Malc . . .

ELOISA

You see, Malcolm, with Madame Girard getting the painting and all, Girard Girard wondered if he couldn't have you. And we told him, naturally, that you were happy here, with us, and our friends, and all, and that we didn't see any reason why *he* should have you when we were all so happy *together.* I mean with Madame Girard coming along and practically stealing your portrait right from under our collective nose—for a song!—and now all we have left *is* you . . .


JEROME

. . . and why would he want to take *that* away from us, too . . .


ELOISA

. . . exactly.


MALCOLM

(*After a short pause; rather unhappy*) Did you *sell* me to him, Jerome? Did you sell me to Mr. Girard?


JEROME

(*Whining*) Aw, now, Malc . . .


ELOISA

(*Rather put out*) I wouldn't put it *that* way, Malcolm. . . .


MALCOLM

How much did you *get* for me, Jerome? (*Jerome fidgets, doesn't answer*) How much did I fetch?


ELOISA

(*To fill an awkward silence*) I'm afraid you didn't do quite as well as your picture, sweetheart. . . .


MALCOLM

(*Sad, but steely*) How much did you sell me for, Jerome?


JEROME

Thirty-five hundred dollars.


MALCOLM

(*Sad, nodding*) I see.

JEROME

You'll be happy with Mr. Girard, Malc.

ELOISA

Oh, you *will*, sweetie!

MALCOLM

(*Tiny voice*) Where am I to go? (*Clears his throat*) I say, where am I to go?

JEROME

He's waiting for you . . .

ELOISA

(*Enthusiastically*) . . . at the entrance to the botanical gardens.

JEROME

(*Soft*) Right now!

ELOISA

Unh-hunh.

MALCOLM

(*Confused, lost*) Well . . . well, I think I'll say goodbye, then.

JEROME

Not goodbye, Malc; au revoir!

ELOISA

You come see us when we get back . . . if we go.

MALCOLM

(*As things fly apart, as the* BRACES *vanish*) Yes, well . . . Goodbye, Jerome the burglar, goodbye, Eloisa Brace. Goodbye. Goodbye. (*Alone*) Sold? Sold to Mr. Girard? Like a

. . . a white slave or something? Well, why not? I mean, I suppose it's as natural as anything in the world. But really! You'd think I could stick . . . somewhere! Sold? SOLD? The . . . THE WHOLE WORLD IS FLYING APART! And . . . what's to become of me? WHAT'S TO BECOME OF ME NOW!!??

# ACT TWO

# SCENE ONE

*(The entrance to the botanical gardens. Daylight.* MALCOLM *asleep.* GUS *enters: tall, brawny, got up in motorcycle uniform; regards* MALCOLM *briefly, kicks him gently)*

GUS

Hey, buddy; hey; hey, you, there.

MALCOLM

*(Waking up, sort of beside himself)* Hm? Hm? Girard Girard, is that . . . ? Oh; excuse me; I'm sorry.

GUS

*(Not unfriendly; just all business)* You a contemporary?

MALCOLM

*(Looking around for* GIRARD GIRARD*)* Have you seen . . . you haven't seen Mr. Girard Girard nearby, have you?

GUS

Don't kid around, buddy.

MALCOLM

*(Very sincere)* Oh, I'm not kidding around. I assure you, I'm quite serious. He was supposed to be here last night, and he and I . . .

GUS

Unh-hunh. I said: you a contemporary?

MALCOLM

*(Ponders it)* A contemporary of *what?*

GUS

*(Not understanding)* What?


MALCOLM

Of *what?*


GUS

*(A little edge to his tone)* I don't know what you talkin' about, mister.


MALCOLM

*(Rubbing his eyes)* Well, I'm afraid I don't know what you're talking about, either.


GUS

*(Shrugs)* Don't matter. If you one of the contemporaries, we go right on over to Melba's. If you ain't, it don't matter too awful much anyhow, on account of you are the *type.*


MALCOLM

*(Rather abstracted)* You don't seem to understand. I came here yesterday afternoon, at the—I suppose I should say invitation—of Mr. Girard Girard—I'm sure you've heard of him—the magnate?


GUS

*(Shaking his head)* Unh-unh.


MALCOLM

Well; I would have thought everybody had.


GUS

*Let's* go.


MALCOLM

*(Rather panicky)* Go! I can't go anywhere, I've been too far

already. You don't know what's happened to me, sir!

GUS

*(Firm, but not ugly)* Stow it, buddy! Now, come on.

MALCOLM

No! I won't! *I can't!*

GUS

You really waiting for anybody?

MALCOLM

*(Small, lost)* I . . . thought I was.

GUS

Unh-hunh. Figgered. Come on, boy.

MALCOLM

*(Being dragged)* Who is . . . who is . . . Melba?

GUS

Melba? You don't know who Melba is?

MALCOLM

I've heard of who Melba was, but this can't possibly be the same lady.

GUS

Where you been living, boy?

MALCOLM

Oh, lots of places.

GUS

An' you never heard of Melba. Well, buddy, you got a pleasure comin'. Melba is a *singer.* And she ain't just any

singer, she is . . . man, she got solid gold records stacked up
like they was dishes.

MALCOLM

(*Quite pleased*) Really?

GUS

You ain't never heard her records? . . . *Hot in the Rocker?*

MALCOLM

N . . . nooo.

GUS

Or, *When You Said Goodbye, Dark Daddy?*

MALCOLM

(*Uncertain*) I . . . don't think so; no.

GUS

Boy! You ain't been anywhere. (*Sings*)
    "When you said goodbye, dark daddy,
    Did you know I'd not yet said hello?"

MALCOLM

(*Somewhat dubious*) That's . . . very catchy.

GUS

She sold eight million of that one.

MALCOLM

(*Fascinated by the high figure, nothing else*) Eight million!
Really!

GUS

Melba gonna like you. Boy, I *hope* she like you. She say to
me, Gus, you go out and find me a contemporary. (*Small
threat*) You better be a contemporary.

MALCOLM

*(Noticing where they're coming to)* Well, I'm bound to be, aren't I, of . . . something.


GUS

*(Shaking his head)* You better be, that's all I gotta say.

# SCENE TWO

(*We have come to the backstage area of the club wherein* MELBA *is performing; we hear screaming from "onstage," and we hear* MELBA *singing, vaguely; what we hear mostly is applause and screaming*)

MALCOLM

Where *are* we?

GUS

You hear that? You hear them people?

MALCOLM

(*Rather put off*) Yes, what . . . what *is* all this?

GUS

(*Proud*) That's Melba. Listen to 'em yellin. Boy! She gets 'em. (*Shouting*) GO TO IT, MELBA, BABY!

MALCOLM

But, where are we?

GUS

Why'n't you sit yourself down wait a bit. GO TO IT, BABY. GIVE IT TO 'EM!

MALCOLM

(*Whining some*) I shouldn't be here; Mr. Girard won't know where to find me, and . . . or anything.

GUS

Melba be offstage soon, you just sit wait on her. (WAITER

*enters)* Hey, Jocko, give us a couple of drinks, now, I brought
me a contemporary.

JOCKO

Usual, Gus?

GUS

Natcherly. What you wanna drink, boy?

MALCOLM

*(To* JOCKO, *sensing he looks familiar)* How do you do? *(To*
GUS*)* I . . . I don't know; I don't drink very . . .

GUS

Two of the usual, Jocko-boy; two big ones. *(*JOCKO *nods, begins to exit)* She knockin'em out, hey?

JOCKO

Right out flat. Two big ones. *(Exits)*
*(The song ends, great screaming, shouting.* MELBA *backs onstage)*

MELBA

All right! All right! Jesus! God, they love me! Give me a
drink. JOCKO!

JOCKO

Here you go, Melba: a big one, the usual.

MELBA

Oh, Jocko baby, you like chimes. *(To them all)* Listen to
those bastards out there. Doesn't that warm the old cockles?
Wow!

JOCKO

They love you, Melba.

MELBA

*(About "them")* Nudnicks.

MALCOLM

*(To* JOCKO*)* Th-thank you.

MELBA

*(Shouting)* ALL RIGHT! I'LL BE OUT! SHUT THE . . . *(Mutters)*
Bums. *(Notices* MALCOLM*)* What you got here, Gus?

JOCKO

*(Exiting)* Something mighty young, Melba.

GUS

Hey, Melba? You asked me to go find you a contemporary.
How's this? He contemporary enough?

MELBA

*(Circles* MALCOLM*)* Hmmmm. What's your name, baby?

MALCOLM

M-Malcolm . . . Melba.

GUS

*(Proud)* He a contemporary or not?

MELBA

*(Still appraising)* Unh-hunh. Yup, that's what it is.

GUS

*(Proud)* I knew I could do it.

MELBA

*(Sitting next to Malcolm, putting her arm on him)* I'm
Melba, honey . . . sweet little Malcolm.

MALCOLM

*(Blushing)* Aw, gee . . .

MELBA

*(Stroking his cheek)* You like me a little bit, Malcolm, baby?

MALCOLM

*(About to say something else, does not, kisses* MELBA's *hand)* I've . . . I've had such a . . . long . . . short . . . life.

MELBA

*(Raises her glass)* To Malcolm, and his long short life. *(Leaning to him)* I could marry you, baby. (MALCOLM *kisses her hand again)*

GUS

You can't get married again, Melba; think of . . .

MELBA

*(Threatening)* That will do, Gus. *(To* MALCOLM, *now)* Gus was my first husband, old number one, as we sometimes call him.

GUS

I'm not ashamed of it, Melba.

MELBA

I'm so glad he found you, baby. *(Kisses* MALCOLM *on the mouth)* Do you think you could find happiness with me? Hunh?

MALCOLM

*(Hesitates briefly, then in tearful, tired relief)* Oh, yes I do, Melba; I really do.

MELBA

*(To* GUS) Isn't it wonderful? Us young people are so . . . are you sulking again? *(No answer; addresses* MALCOLM *again)* Would you marry me, Malcolm?

GUS

*(Some anguish)* It's too sudden. Wait till Thursday, or somethin'.

MELBA

*(To* MALCOLM*)* Do you really care for me? I mean, honest-really?

MALCOLM

*(Slowly, seriously)* I . . . I do, Melba. I've lost so much. *(Kisses her on the throat, impulsively)* I DO, MELBA: I DO!

MELBA

I have never been so quickly surprised, or so quickly happy. *(To* GUS; *rather ugly)* You begrudge me this happiness, don't you! You begrudge me this tiny, tiny bit of happiness in my life of pettiness and struggle. . . .

GUS

Melba, honey, happiness is the last thing I begrudge you, but I don't want you to rush into matrimony this here time; think of all the other times you done got stung. Think of the courts, Melba, honey.

MELBA

*(To* MALCOLM*)* He begrudges me. *(Snuggles)* God, we'll be happy—for a long, long time.

MALCOLM

*(A gurgling sound, resembling a coo)* Rrrooooooooo. *(Sits up, startled)*

MELBA

Isn't he beautiful, Gus? You notice the dimples when he smiles. *(Snuggles again)* Aw, *sweet*heart!

MALCOLM

Rrrrooooooo. But *you're* beautiful, Melba. You're the . . . beautiful one.

MELBA

And you really feel you want to marry me, dearest?

GUS

(*A cry of pain*) MELBA, SWEET JESUS!!

MELBA

(*To* MALCOLM) He's carrying a torch, sweetheart; don't pay any attention to him.

MALCOLM

(*Stammering*) You're . . . my girl . . . Melba.

MELBA

(*Sighing happily*) I've simply got it is all; it's come like lightning, and . . . well, I've been got.

GUS

I may be carryin' a torch, Melba, honey, but SWEET JESUS, HE AIN'T OLD ENOUGH!!

MELBA

(*Stopping* MALCOLM's *ears*) Don't listen to him; jealousy and rage, that's all it is. Six weeks of marriage teaches you an awful lot about a man. But *our* marriage, Malcolm, will last on, and on . . . precious.

MALCOLM

(*About to swoon with joy*) Oh, Melba!

MELBA

(*Rising, more businesslike*) Good boy. Now, I gotta go out and sing some more, sing for our wedding supper, babyface.

MALCOLM

But . . . but, Melba!

MELBA

No buts, baby. Momma gotta work.


MALCOLM

Aw, Melba . . .


MELBA

*(Hand on hip)* Well, of course, I *could* quit my career, honey, and you could go out run telegrams or something.


MALCOLM

*(Little boy)* I . . . I understand, Melba.


MELBA

*(Effusive again)* Aw, give me a kiss, sweetheart. *(Engulfs* MALCOLM *again, kisses him lots)*


MALCOLM

Rrrrrrrooooooo.


MELBA

You hear those bastards out there? They're my public, angel-face, those nogoods. You my private. See ya Thursday, hunh?


MALCOLM

*(Very serious)* Till . . . till Thursday . . . Melba.


MELBA

Bye, sweetpants. *(As the crowd sounds increase)* I'M COMING! YA BUMS! *(To* MALCOLM, *kissing him one last time)* Gus'll take real good care of you, baby. *(To* GUS*)* Gus, you take real good care of, uh, Malcolm here, ya hear? *(Waving at* MAL- COLM, *blowing him a kiss. Sotto voce to* GUS, *taking money from her bodice, giving it to* GUS*)* Mature him up a little, you know? You know what I mean? Mature him up a little. *(*MELBA *exits, the crowd sounds swell.)*

# ENTRE-SCENE

(GUS *and* MALCOLM *walking, the last scene having faded*)

GUS

(*Shaking his head*) I don't know; I just don't know.

MALCOLM

(*Lost little boy*) Gus? . . . What have I done?

GUS

(*Talking more or less to himself*) Mature him up a little bit, she says. Mature him up! How the hell I gonna do that, hunh?

MALCOLM

Gus? What have I done?

GUS

Hm?

MALCOLM

What have I done?

GUS

What have you done!? You have got yourself engaged to Melba baby, that what you done.

MALCOLM

I don't under*stand.*

GUS

(*Remembering*) She sure is a knockout, hunh?

MALCOLM

I mean, I've never *felt* like that before, and everything happened so quickly, and . . .

GUS

Bang! it hits! Unh? The old kazamm; pow!

MALCOLM

(*Wonder*) But I just met her, and . . .

GUS

Well, you get a chance to get to know her some.

MALCOLM

It's . . . it's being so close to her like that . . . when she . . . hugs and everything.

GUS

(*Pained*) Don't talk about it, boy.

MALCOLM

(*Blushing*) And . . . and when she kisses and all . . .

GUS

(*Anguish*) Just *don't!* Don't *stir* me.

MALCOLM

. . . and everything happens, and . . .

GUS

(*Returning slowly to businesslike stature*) An' . . . an' now we gotta mature you up some. (*Shows* MALCOLM *the money*) See this? This is money to mature you up, boy. Now, look, Malco-boy, I gotta ask you a plain question.

MALCOLM

(*Nodding happily*) Yes.

GUS

To put it delicate-like, boy, have you ever been completely and solidly joined to a woman? Have you ever been joined to a woman the way nature meant? Yes or no.

MALCOLM

(*After a puzzled pause*) Well, it's always been so very dark— where I was—and people were—shifting so . . .

GUS

I can see you ain't, and that's what Melba meant—what she sent us out for, to mature you up.

# SCENE THREE

(*Set comes on. Sign saying* PRIVATE AND TURKISH BATHS. CABI-
NETS AND OVERNIGHT COTTAGES. $2.00)

GUS

You see that place over there? That's where I'm gonna take
you: Rosita's. Madame Rosita they used to call her. You
heard of her?

MALCOLM

(*Shakes his head*) No.

GUS

You ain't heard of anything! Well, that's what I'm here for.
(*Mumbles*) That what sweet Melba told me t'do—get you
ready. . . .

MALCOLM

(*A little confused*) You're . . . you're very kind, Gus.

GUS

(*Gives* MALCOLM *a funny look; calls*) Hey, Miles, Miles? (*A
seedy man comes out, green visor; played by the actor who
plays* COX) Miles? How you doin', boy?

MILES

Gus, is that really you? Well, I'll be damned. (*Looks at* MAL-
COLM, *who is staring at him, open-mouthed*) Where'd you get
him—the one with his mouth hangin' open?

MALCOLM

(*Rather hurt*) But, Mr. Cox!

MILES

*(It is not* cox, *of course)* Name is Miles, boy. Gus, how long's it been?

GUS

*(Bringing out the money)* Need some work done, Miles; quick and special.

MALCOLM

*(Very hurt)* Mr. Cox!

MILES

*(Very straight)* That ain't my name, boy. Work, Gus?

GUS

*(Yawning)* Yeah, house special for the boy.

MILES

*(Looks at* MALCOLM *dubiously)* I was just wonderin' if you'd noticed this kid here is sorta young.

GUS

*(Waves the money under* MILES' *nose)* Oh, I don't know.

MILES

Yeah, well, looks is deceiving.

GUS

He gonna marry Melba.

MILES

Hunh! Who ain't!

MALCOLM

*(Offended)* Please!

GUS

(*To* MALCOLM) Now, upstairs is where you're gonna go, kiddie. When you through, you come down here an' wake me up. Which is my room, Miles?

MILES

(*Counting the money*) You pick one out; nobody here tonight at all.

GUS

O.K., I take me old number twenty-two. (*To* MALCOLM) You got that, boy? Twenty-two.

MALCOLM

(*Shivering a little*) R-right.
     (*Enters a woman of indeterminate age, a parody of
     a whore; to be played by the actress who plays
     LAUREEN*)

ROSITA

Gus! Baby! It's been years! (*Goes to embrace him*)

GUS

It's the boy this time, uh, sweetheart. I just gonna get me a shower and a snooze; I ain't had no sleep in a week, if you know what I mean.

ROSITA

Let me get this all down. You are sending *him* . . . upstairs for *you*.

GUS

Break him in, for Christ's sake, will ya?

MALCOLM

(*A little scared*) I could swear I know you, madame.

GUS

*(To* MALCOLM; *weary)* You do like I told you now, back in the street. I want you to go through it all just like I told you nature meant.

ROSITA

*(Gives* GUS *a quiet raspberry; says to* MALCOLM*)* O.K., you come on with me, honey. *(Begins dragging* MALCOLM *off)*

GUS

*(To* MALCOLM *as he is exited)* An' don't you come back down without you had it, you hear?

MALCOLM

*(Being exited)* Had . . . had what!

ROSITA

Come on.

MILES

*(Shakes his head; laughs)* Jesus!

GUS

*(Chuckling)* Poor baby boy.

MILES

Gonna shack up with Melba, hunh?

GUS

Weddin' bells and all. *(Moving off, slowly, wearily)* Oh, I tell you, Miles, I am so weary, so sad. . . . I think I'll lie down, not wake up again. Wouldn't matter . . . 'cept for the kid, there.

MILES

*(As they exit)* How old *is* he?

GUS

Malco? I don't know: fourteen, fifteen, maybe. Don't matter:
Melba'll age him up a little.

(MILES *and* GUS *have exited*)

# SCENE FOUR

(MALCOLM *and* ROSITA *come on,* MALCOLM *carrying the locket*)

ROSITA

Well, goodbye and God bless, kiddie. You're the real stuff.

MALCOLM

Gee, thanks, Rosita.

ROSITA

You've made an old woman very happy. (*She exits as soon as possible*)

MALCOLM

(*Left alone, joyous*) Melba? Melba? (MELBA *appears, way down right, say, with open arms*)

MELBA

Here I am, baby. Come to Momma!

MALCOLM

(*Going to her, puppylike enthusiasm*) I . . . I did it, Melba, all the way through . . . three times! Wow! It looks like I'll be a bridegroom after all.

MELBA

(*Pleased*) Yeah?

MALCOLM

Yes, and Madame Rosita paid me a compliment; she said I was the real stuff, and she gave me tea . . . in between . . . and when we were all done she gave me this locket, which has a real, little tiny American flag all rolled up inside.

MELBA

Yeah; that's great. Let's go to Chicago, baby!

MALCOLM

But . . . but why?

MELBA

You ever been married in Chicago?

MALCOLM

Well . . . no!

MELBA

Well, neither have I, baby! Let's go! *(They race off together)*

# ENTRE-SCENE

(*Another no-set promenade.* MADAME GIRARD *comes on, followed by* KERMIT; *they stroll*)

MADAME GIRARD

(*Not looking at* KERMIT *as they walk;* KERMIT *keeps eyeing her, with a set mouth and mistrustful eyes*) I understand—though one is never sure of one's information in a world of gossips—that they were married in Chicago. Would you like a peppermint? No? That they were married in Chicago, by some defrocked justice of the peace—a scandal, if you care for my opinion—stop eyeing me—that they flew to the Caribbean for a honeymoon which was interrupted by their having to move from hotel to hotel, country to country, that they have returned here, where that loathsome brat of a chanteuse has resumed her career of caterwauling, and that Malcolm—that poor, dear child—walk with me, can you?—is virtually a prisoner in some den she keeps. (*Sobs*) I have written *letters!* I have *tele*phoned! My calls have been answered by a manservant who sounds Cuban at the least, and my letters! Stop staring at me! My letters have been returned to me, unopened, with semi-literate notes, scrawled by that girl Svengali, informing me that Malcolm—oh, dear God, child, come back to me!—is busy at being married, is too occupied and happy to be, as she puts it, dragged under by his past! If you will not walk like a proper companion, we shall both stand still. (*They stand still*) Too occupied! Too happy! Dear Lord, can people be that? (KERMIT *stands in front of her, rather like a bulldog about to spring*) Are you going to bite me? You?—you who ruined everything? You who cringed when we came to take you with us? You, but for whom we should all be together now, Malcolm with us? Malcolm's pic-

ture! His picture stares at me, and tells me, "It is not I, dear
Madame Girard, not I. Not I, dear Madame Girard, not I."
I can't look at it any more! It is *not* my Malcolm. Help me!
Help me, please! Get me my Malcolm back! (KERMIT *starts
walking off*) Wait! Help me! Dearest Kermit! Wait! *(She
exits after him)*

# SCENE FIVE

(As MADAME GIRARD *exits, we hear* MALCOLM *and* MELBA
*giggling, she shrieking a little, too. Lights come up on* MAL-
COLM *in bed, naked to the waist, or wearing pajamas, depending on the build of the actor playing the part.* MELBA *in a
negligee, on the bed beside him.* MELBA *is tickling him*)


MALCOLM

(*Very ticklish, speaks between giggles*) Melba . . . honey
. . . please . . . Melba . . .


MELBA

How's my kitchy-koo? Kitchy-kitchy-kitchy? Hmmmm?


MALCOLM

(A *cry-giggle*) MMMM EEEEELLLLLBBBBB AAAAA.


MELBA

Kitchy-kitchy-kitchy? Aw, sweetheart. (*Kisses him all over*)
Aw, baby. Come to Melba.


MALCOLM

(*Giggles subsiding some*) Aw, honest, Melba, I love you; I do.


MELBA

(*Seriously, sensuously; hand on his crotch*) Oh, I do love you,
too, sweet pants. Yes, I do. . . . You have *got* it, baby; you
have got what Melba wants.


MALCOLM

We . . . do an awful lot of being married, don't we, Melba?

MELBA

*(Eyes closed)* Oooooh, you are good at marriage, sweetheart, yes, you are. Gimme that mouth of yours, tonguey-boy. Ummmmmmmm. *(Kisses him fervently)* Oh baby let's do marriage right this second sweetheart lover baby dollface, c'mon, c'MON!

MALCOLM

*(Seeing that* HELIODORO, *the Cuban valet, has entered with a tray of coffee)* Uh, Melba . . .

MELBA

C'mon, sweetpants, let's get some action goin'. . . .

MALCOLM

Uh . . . good—good morning, Heliodoro.

MELBA

Hunh? *(Sees* HELIODORO) What the hell do you want?

HELIODORO

*(Who is played by one of the* YOUNG MEN) Coffee; coffee time.

MELBA

Nuts! It's take the frigging coffee and get the hell out of the bedroom time; that's what time it is.

MALCOLM

I'd . . . *(timidly)* . . . I'd like some coffee, Melba, and . . . and maybe some breakfast? Breakfast, too?

MELBA

*(Mock tough)* Married six weeks, an' he's cold as a stone. Look at 'im. *(Cuddles)* Baby want breakfast?

MALCOLM

Just . . . just a little.

MELBA

*(Gets up off the bed, stretches, shows off a little for* HELIO-
DORO*)* O.K. Momma got to go to work anyway. But you stay
right there, sweetheart; you just lie there an' read a funny-
book, or somethin', so Momma know where you are when
she want you. O.K.?

MALCOLM

*(So smitten)* I'll . . . be right here where you want me,
Melba.

MELBA

Right on top, baby! That's where I want you. Hey, don't
forget, hotrocks, we're goin' out clubbin' tonight after I get
done work.

MALCOLM

*(Small protest in this)* We go . . . to a nightclub *every* night,
Melba. At least one.

MELBA

*(To a child)* Well, I'm proud of my baby. *(To* HELIODORO*)*
Fix him a Bloody Mary or somethin', will you?

HELIODORO

Maybe he shouldn't drink so . . .

MELBA

*(Murderous)* Fix him a goddam Bloody Mary! *(Blows* MAL-
COLM *a kiss)* See you, sweetheart. *(Exits)*

HELIODORO

You want coffee?

MALCOLM

Yes, please, and . . . I don't need a Bloody Mary, O.K.?
Some . . . eggs and toast and bacon, and . . .

HELIODORO

You gettin' thin.

MALCOLM

(*Sweet and innocent*) Melba says marriage is a thinning business.

HELIODORO

(*Shrugs*) I suppose she oughta know.

MALCOLM

Have you been married, Heliodoro?

HELIODORO

(*Laughs*) Me? No, I'm too young.

MALCOLM

How old *are* you?

HELIODORO

Twenty-two.

MALCOLM

(*Sad*) Yes, that's very young. (*Brightly*) I'm . . . fifteen, I think.

HELIODORO

(*Changing the subject*) That . . . that lady called again today.

MALCOLM

(*Some gloom*) I don't know why Melba won't let me see Madame Girard or . . . or anybody . . . any of my friends. I . . . well, I love Melba like all get out, and everything . . . but . . . I get lonely . . . just being here like this.

HELIODORO

(*A little embarrassed*) You . . . you want to start your Bloody Marys?

MALCOLM

(*Weary; head back on pillow*) I suppose so; I suppose I'd better if Melba thinks I should.


HELIODORO

I'll bring you a Bloody Mary.


MALCOLM

(*Weary*) I suppose you should: I've got a long, hard day
ahead of me.

(FADE)

# ENTRE-SCENE

(ELOISA *and* JEROME *come on, huffily, pursued by* GIRARD GIRARD. *No set needed; this* can *be in the nature of a promenade*)

ELOISA

I have never been so insulted; never, in my long and scrabby life—the life of an artist, always hurt, always wanting—have I been so insulted. Jerome? Don't talk to the man.

GIRARD GIRARD

But my dear Mrs. Brace . . .

ELOISA

Never.

GIRARD GIRARD

(*Both of the others are huffily silent. Reasoning*) I have come to you, beseeching, a humble man, casting about in the dark . . .

ELOISA

You have not! You came in here, you came upon us, near-*flagrante*, howling your insults. . . .

GIRARD GIRARD

I DID NO SUCH THING!

ELOISA

(*Snappish; for confirmation*) Jerome?

JEROME

Never, in all my years behind bars . . .

GIRARD GIRARD

*(Anguish)* Where is Malcolm? Please!

ELOISA

Hah! Accusing us again, are you?

GIRARD GIRARD

*(Patient)* I have accused you of nothing, my good woman. I merely explained that I had a business matter of some urgency to settle and when I arrived at the botanical gardens, some hours later than I had intended to . . .

ELOISA

He'd gone!

GIRARD GIRARD

Yes!

ELOISA

And that *we* had stolen him!

GIRARD GIRARD

No!

JEROME

*(Sneering)* We heard you.

GIRARD GIRARD

I suggested no such thing!

ELOISA

We may be poor . . .

JEROME

. . . and I may have a record a yard long, but . . .

GIRARD GIRARD

WHERE IS MALCOLM!?

ELOISA

(*Sniffs. After a tiny pause*) I'm sure we don't know.

JEROME

(*Oily*) It's out of our hands, buddy; we delivered the merchandise, free and clear, good condition; we don't take no responsibility for . . .

GIRARD GIRARD

Please! I must have him!

ELOISA

(*Grand*) It would seem to me that if you're careless enough to . . . abandon the child under some bushes somewhere while you go about your filthy moneymaking . . .

JEROME

. . . that it's hardly our affair.

ELOISA

We did not steal him.

GIRARD GIRARD

(*Sad, defeated*) I . . . I merely wondered.

ELOISA

Well, we . . . we have problems enough of our own, without running any sort of . . .

GIRARD GIRARD

*If* . . . if he returns to you . . .

ELOISA

There you go again.

JEROME

Prison was nothing! The unimaginable indignities of the

cell block were . . . were frolic next to . . . to your vile
and tawdry suggestion, sir.

### GIRARD GIRARD

Jerome, I merely . . .

### ELOISA

Never! Tell me this, Girard Girard: do you think your wealth
entitles you? Do you?

### JEROME

The older prisoners, after lights out, making straight for the
cells where the younger inmates cower, their rough blankets
pulled over their heads . . .

### GIRARD GIRARD

My dear friends . . .

### ELOISA

La vie de Boheme, Girard Girard, may indeed seem loose
and unprincipled to some, but . . .

### JEROME

. . . or the entrapments in the shower room, two or three,
coming at you . . . lathered bodies, all glistening, slow
smiles . . .

### ELOISA

(*An aside*) Control yourself, Jerome.

# SCENE SIX

(To one side of the stage, a nightclub table, with MALCOLM and MELBA at it, both noticeably drunk. Lots of noise in the background, music, chattering)

MELBA

You like rum sours, baby?

MALCOLM

I would seem to, Melba-honey. This is number . . . what?

MELBA

Who cares? Drink up.

MALCOLM

(Notices MELBA open a vial) Melba, what is that stuff you're always putting in our drinks and all?

MELBA

(Pouring some in their drinks) Magic, sweetheart, magic; makes you feel all athletic when we get home, right?

MALCOLM

(Giggles sillily) Right, baby.

MELBA

And, of course, I didn't marry you for your mind.

MALCOLM

(Drunken pondering) I . . . noticed that.

MELBA

You're gettin' awful thin, big boy. I *like* you thin, you understand, but I suppose I'd like you fat, too.


MALCOLM

(*Puppydog*) I . . . I like you, too, Melba-pussy.


MELBA

(*Abrupt, faintly histrionic*) Don't call me that; number three called me that; it's sacred.


MALCOLM

What is?


MELBA

(*Embarrassed at the sacredness; almost whispers it*) Melba-pussy.


MALCOLM

(*Laughs*) Well, what shall I call you? Melba-puppy? (*Laughs greatly, happily*) Melba-puppy?


MELBA

You're annoying, kiddie, you really are.


MALCOLM

(*Having noticed a* MAN *walk across the stage to a dark area*) That's HE . . . THAT'S MY FATHER! (*Rises*)


MELBA

Sit down, baby.


MALCOLM

(*Moving to go after the* MAN) THAT'S MY FATHER.

MELBA

*(Sharp)* Come back here, Malcolm!


MALCOLM

*(Unrestrainable, moving to the other side of the stage)* THAT'S MY FATHER!

# SCENE SEVEN

*(The area on* MELBA *blacks out, and the lights come up on the* MAN, *in a washroom, facing the audience, washing his hands at a basin)*

MALCOLM

*(Stretching his arms out to the* MAN, *weaving a little)* Father! Where did you go all this time? *(The* MAN *either touches his hair or his mustache, does not reply or take notice of* MAL-COLM) Don't you *recognize me? I'd . . . I'd recognize* you anywhere. *(Still no response from the* MAN) Father! *(Goes up to him, puts his arm on his shoulder)* Please, father . . .

MAN

*(Looks straight at* MALCOLM, *no recognition; cold)* Would you allow me to pass?

MALCOLM

You're . . . you're pretending not to recognize me! Is it . . . is it because I married Melba, or because I left the bench, or because I . . .

MAN

*(Making an effort to get by)* Allow me to pass!

MALCOLM

*(Starting to grapple with the* MAN; *the struggle gets hotter)* Please, father! It's me! It's Malcolm!

MAN

Help! Help!

MALCOLM

*(Grappling)* Please, father! I've missed you so, and I've been so lonely, and . . .

MAN

*(Struggling)* Let go of me!

MALCOLM

*(In tears now)* Father! Father!

*(The* MAN *seizes* MALCOLM *and throws him hard;* MALCOLM *either hits the washbasin or the floor, heavily. An* ATTENDANT *enters, played by the actor who plays* COX*)*

MAN

*(Pointing to the crumpled* MALCOLM*)* Have that child arrested. He attacked me!

MALCOLM

*(Weeping, from the floor)* Father, I am Malcolm!

MAN

Indeed! *(Turns on his heel, walks into blackness)*

ATTENDANT

Well, now, what's going on? *(*MALCOLM *babbles a few thank yous as the attendant helps him to a sitting position)*

MALCOLM

Melba? Have you seen my wife, sir?

ATTENDANT

*(Incredulous)* You? Are married?

MALCOLM

*(Cheerful through the pain)* Yes, sir! Would you like to meet my wife?

ATTENDANT

*(Examining* MALCOLM's *head)* You're bleeding, boy.

MALCOLM

I . . . I am?

ATTENDANT

That's quite a cut.

MALCOLM

My father refused to recognize me.

ATTENDANT

Who?

MALCOLM

My . . . my father.

ATTENDANT

That couldn't have been your father, sonny.

MALCOLM

N-no?

ATTENDANT

That old pot's been coming here for years. He's nobody's father.

MALCOLM

I . . . I thought it was my father.

ATTENDANT

Better get you home, kid. You don't look so hot.

MALCOLM

Maybe . . . maybe my father . . . never existed.

ATTENDANT

Who knows, son? Better get you to a doctor before you
bleed to death, or something.

MALCOLM

Maybe he never existed at all!

# SCENE EIGHT

(MADAME GIRARD *and* HELIODORO *walk on. They are moving toward the solarium*)

MADAME GIRARD

(*All camp is gone from here to the end of the play*) I apologize to you, young man, if I have bothered you with my calls, my constant ringing.

HELIODORO

That's O.K.

MADAME GIRARD

My search for the one decent thing in this entire world.

HELIODORO

It's O.K.

MADAME GIRARD

Where is my Malcolm? And where is that girl?

HELIODORO

She—an' you mean, I think, great Melba-baby—is with the doctor.

MADAME GIRARD

Why was I not told until now?

HELIODORO

You wanna come in the solarium?

MADAME GIRARD

Of course I want to come into the solarium. My God, what

a bright solarium! Where *is* she? Where is that filthy girl?

#### HELIODORO
(*Embarrassed*) You better watch who you talkin' about, buddy.

(MELBA *enters*)

#### MADAME GIRARD
Is that her?

#### HELIODORO
She call you filthy, baby.

#### MELBA
(*Indifferent*) Yeah? Go fix us a drink. (*As* HELIODORO *hangs back*) Well, go on, kiddo.

#### HELIODORO
I don't wanna leave you here with her, baby.

#### MELBA
Aw, go be a sweetheart and go get us a drink, hunh?

#### MADAME GIRARD
Keep your hands off the servants. You are a married woman, if you care to remember.

#### HELIODORO
See? (*Exits*)

#### MELBA
(*Braying*) Yeah? Well, look here, Madame Hotsy-Totsy, or whatever your name used to be . . .

#### MADAME GIRARD
IS!

MELBA

I been married a few times, you know? And I know how
to act.

MADAME GIRARD

Have pity on us human beings, please!

MELBA

What do you want, a job or something? You looking for
work?

MADAME GIRARD

I am looking for Malcolm!

MELBA

Yeah? Well, I got him, lady; move on.

MADAME GIRARD

I can have you arrested, you know that?

MELBA

Get the hell out of here, will . . .

MADAME GIRARD

THE CHILD IS FIFTEEN YEARS OLD!!!!

MELBA

GET OUT!!

MADAME GIRARD

I warn you, youngish woman, if there is so much as one hair
of his precious head that I find damaged, you'll rue the day
you ever took it on yourself to . . .

MELBA

*(Really beside herself)* GET OUT!!!!

MADAME GIRARD

*(While the* DOCTOR *is entering)* THERE ARE THINGS IN THIS LIFE

WHICH MAY NOT BE PERMITTED!! *(Sees him)* Are you the
doctor?

DOCTOR

I am.

MADAME GIRARD

How is my Malcolm!?

DOCTOR

Are you family?

MADAME GIRARD

I am more than family.

DOCTOR

*(Picking his words carefully)* He . . . is beyond human care.
(MADAME GIRARD *stifles a cry.*)

MELBA

*(Dryly, after a moment)* What do you mean, buddy?

DOCTOR

*(Looking at neither of them)* The child is dying.

MADAME GIRARD

DYING!!

MELBA

*(Pause)* Don't be stupid.

DOCTOR

There is nothing that can be done: give him rest, a bed to
himself, quiet. He is very near death.

MADAME GIRARD

You are a *quack!*

DOCTOR

I may have seen better days, lady, but I know dying when I look at it.

MELBA

(*Clears her throat*) Uh, what is my Malcolm-baby dying of?

MADAME GIRARD

(*Hoping to make it true*) This man doesn't know what he's talking about. People like Malcolm do not die: there isn't room for it.

MELBA

(*Rather harsh*) What's he dying of, hunh?

DOCTOR

(*Reticent*) The . . . young man . . . is dying of a combination of acute alcoholism and, uh, sexual hyperaesthesia, to put it simply.

MADAME GIRARD

(*A command*) NO!

MELBA

(*To the doctor; wincing a little*) I, uh, didn't get you, baby.

MADAME GIRARD

(*Turning full, loss and sickened wrath on* MELBA) You . . . ! you . . . WANTON! Malcolm? MALCOLM? (*Runs off into the blackness*)

DOCTOR

(*Repeating it, mumbling some*) Acute alcoholism and sexual hyperaesthesia: the combination of the two . . . well, one would be enough, but . . .

MELBA

(*Trying to avoid it, quite nervous*) Look, uh, what is this . . .

this sexual stuff, hunh? I mean, he's only been with me,
and . . .

DOCTOR

Sexual hyperaesthesia?

MELBA

Uh, yeah; that.

DOCTOR

Sexual hperaesthesia is, or can be more easily described as,
a violent protracted excess of sexual intercourse. (MELBA *just
stares at him*) I can give you a prescription . . . for the
child . . . useless, of course. . . . (*Sees the answer is "no,"
shrugs, exits*)

HELIODORO

(*Who is entering as the* DOCTOR *exits*) You O.K., baby?
(MELBA *is just standing there, swaying a little*) Hey . . .
Melba . . . you O.K.?

MELBA

(*Preoccupied, a little sad, but calm*) Hunh? (*Puts her hand
out for his*) Hey, give me a hand, will ya, sweetie? This just
ain't a good day. Old Malcolm's gonna die. He's gonna
leave us.

HELIODORO

(*Quiet surprise*) Yeah? (*They exit*)

# SCENE NINE

*(Malcolm's bedroom.* MALCOLM *propped up on pillows, pale, half-conscious. The room in near-darkness.* MADAME GIRARD *enters, hesitantly, comes to the bed)*

MADAME GIRARD

Malcolm? Malcolm? Can I help?

MALCOLM

*(Little boy)* Is it . . . true? Am I going to die?

MADAME GIRARD

*(Not looking at him; softly)* Well . . . who is to say?

MALCOLM

*(Home truth)* You.

MADAME GIRARD

I . . . suspect it may be so.

MALCOLM

*(Sits up in bed, says, with great force)* BUT I'M NOT EVEN TWENTY! IT'S . . . NOT BEEN TWENTY YEARS!

MADAME GIRARD

*(Easing him back to the pillows)* Malcolm . . . please.

MALCOLM

*(Lying back, a little delirious)* I've . . . lost so much, I've . . . lost so very much. (MADAME GIRARD *gets up, moves a little away, doesn't look at* MALCOLM*)* And . . . everyone has . . . swept by . . . Kermit and, and Mr. Girard . . .

(MADAME GIRARD *stiffens a little*) . . . and even Mr. Cox
. . . (*She thinks to speak; does not*) . . . and . . . my father . . . my FATHER! . . . What . . . (*softly*) what have I
not lost?

MADAME GIRARD

(*Waits, expecting more, nodding. Waits, suddenly realizes,
turns*) No . . . (*shakes her head*) . . . no . . . PRINCE!
(*Goes to the bed, touches him, takes her hand away*) Say
. . . say more. . . . There's more. (*Begins to cry*) There's
. . . much, much more. More, Oh, Malcolm . . . oh, child.
My Malcolm. What have you not lost? . . . And I . . .
And all . . . What have *we* not lost? What, indeed. Did
none of us ever care? (*The others start coming on, will group
near, around, behind the bed*) You, my poor husband, with
that woman you choose to call your wife? Or you? Or you?
Or even you. Malcolm is dead.

KERMIT

Malcolm? Dead?

LAUREEN

Dead?

ELOISA

Just like that?

JEROME

(*Quiet awe*) Wow.

MADAME GIRARD

No, not just like that.

COX

I suppose he didn't have the stuff, that's all. God knows,
I tried.

MADAME GIRARD

Oh, yes, we tried . . . we all tried.

MALCOLM

I'm . . . I'm cold.

MADAME GIRARD

And you, my husband? Silent?

GIRARD GIRARD

(*Considerable pain*) Let it go, my dear. He . . . he passed
through so quickly; none of us could grasp hold.

LAUREEN

*We* tried.

ELOISA

Sure; we tried.

JEROME

Sure.

LAUREEN

He was a sweet kid.

KERMIT

I tried . . . as much as I could.

COX

He didn't have the stuff, that's all.

MADAME GIRARD

None of you . . . ever cared. (*She senses they want to leave*)
I shall have a funeral for him! A silver casket? Banks of
roses and violets? Thousands and thousands of . . . and a
gilded hearse? With black-plumed horses?

### GIRARD GIRARD

Let it go, my dear.

### LAUREEN

Yes, let it go.

### MADAME GIRARD

None of you . . . ever cared. None of you. *(They begin to fade)*

### ELOISA

We cared, dear.

### JEROME

Sure, we cared.

### LAUREEN

Of course we did, dear.

### KERMIT

I cared . . . as much as I could.

### GIRARD GIRARD

Let it go, my dear.

### COX

He . . . he didn't have the stuff . . . that's all.

### MADAME GIRARD

*(Isolated now)* You . . . you can come and see his portrait . . . if you care. It's . . . not much. But . . . it will have to do. That's all that's left. Just that. Nothing more. Nothing more. Just that.

*(As the lights fade on* MADAME GIRARD *and the dead* MAL-COLM, *they rise on the golden bench, high on a platform, above and behind. The bench is suffused in a golden light for a few moments, then all fades to blackness)*

# JAMES PURDY

*James Purdy, author, born in Ohio, first emerged as a writer of importance in 1957 when his book of stories,* COLOR OF DARKNESS, *was published. His novel* MALCOLM (1959) *has come to be considered an American classic, translated into twelve languages.* THE NEPHEW (1960) *and his savage satire on American values,* CABOT WRIGHT BEGINS (1964), *have established his reputation as one of the most original of contemporary writers in the English language. Some of his stories were presented in an off-Broadway production in 1962 under the title* COLOR OF DARKNESS.

# EDWARD ALBEE

*Edward Albee, playwright, was born March 12, 1928, and began writing plays thirty years later. His plays are, in order of composition,* THE ZOO STORY, THE DEATH OF BESSIE SMITH, THE SANDBOX, THE AMERICAN DREAM, WHO'S AFRAID OF VIRGINIA WOOLF?, THE BALLAD OF THE SAD CAFÉ, TINY ALICE *and* MALCOLM. *He is presently at work on two plays,* A DELICATE BALANCE *and* THE SUBSTITUTE SPEAKER.